The BOY on a
BLACK HORSE

BOOKS BY
*N*ANCY *S*PRINGER

Not on a White Horse
They're All Named Wildfire
Red Wizard
The Friendship Song
The Boy on a Black Horse

The BOY on a BLACK HORSE

NANCY SPRINGER

ATHENEUM 1994 NEW YORK
Maxwell Macmillan Canada
Toronto
Maxwell Macmillan International
New York Oxford Singapore Sydney

Atheneum
Macmillan Publishing Company
866 Third Avenue
New York, NY 10022

Maxwell Macmillan Canada, Inc.
1200 Eglinton Avenue East
Suite 200
Don Mills, Ontario M3C 3N1

Macmillan Publishing Company is part of the Maxwell Communication Group of Companies.

First edition

Printed in the United States of America

10 9 8 7 6 5 4 3 2 1

The text of this book is set in 12-point Caslon 224 Book.

Library of Congress Cataloging-in-Publication Data
Springer, Nancy.
The boy on a black horse / by Nancy Springer. —1st ed.
p.   cm.
Summary: Intrigued by the mysterious and angry Romany boy who joins her class, thirteen-year-old Gray finds that she shares her love of horses but harbors a dark secret.
ISBN 0–689–31840–5
[1. Gypsies—Fiction. 2. Horses—Fiction. 3. Child abuse—Fiction.]
I. Title.
PZ7.S76846Bo   1994   92–27158
[Fic]—dc20

The *B*OY *on a* *B*LACK *H*ORSE

CHAPTER

— 1 —

The first time I ever saw him I was pretending to write in my daily journal in language arts class but actually drawing a horse—the head and neck had come out run-in-the-wind gorgeous, but I knew I would never get the rest of it as good—and when the door opened I looked up like everybody else, and there was a strange boy walking into my life.

This is his story really, not mine. Though it kind of turns into my story.

Something about him cut me open like a knife. He wasn't tall, and he wasn't good-looking—in fact, his face was crooked and his skin was marked up like it had been through a lot. But there was something about the fierce way he moved that went straight to my heart. He was dressed all in black. And his black hair hung wild, like the wind had been in it. And his fierce dark eyes looked wild. I knew right then I was going to care about

1

him—not like a boyfriend; I didn't think I was ever going to have a boyfriend or a husband like other girls, and I still don't—but I knew I was going to care about what happened to him.

Mrs. Higby stood up behind her desk, and by the way her third chin was jumping around I saw she was scared of him. "Who have we here?" she said with her voice way up in her nose. Mrs. Higby is always "we," like she was more than one person, when really one of her is plenty, thank you.

The new boy gave her his yellow slip from the office. She looked at it like she couldn't read it. "What is this name?"

"Chav." His voice was gritty and low.

"We beg your pardon?"

"Chav." He said it like "Shah," like he was the king of some foreign country. And the way he stood there, carrying himself tall and airy with his head high, he could have been.

"Spell it."

He did. She wrote on the yellow slip. "Chav." She couldn't pronounce it the way he did. "And this last name?"

He shrugged.

"We need to know your last name for the records."

He told her a last name, but it could not have been his real name. It was a joke only an adult would miss. Kids burst out laughing because they thought he was being a smart-ass and yanking her chain, but he wasn't. His face didn't smirk back at the laughter—it might as well have been carved out of rough brown rock. He did not care whether people laughed or what they were laughing at.

Mrs. Higby was peering at him through her bifocals, not sure whether to believe him. She said, "Spell it."

He did, straight-faced. Mrs. Higby still could not tell about him, and neither could I—what was he trying to prove? I was not laughing, but some of the boys in class were laughing so hard they were kicking the furniture.

"Class!" Mrs. Higby screeched, and she gave up on Chav. "Sit there!" she ordered him, and he took the front-row desk across the room from me. His black hair hung down in his eyes. He tossed his head and flung it back, like a wild stallion tossing his forelock.

Mrs. Higby told us to put our journals away and got us going on the lesson. We were each to have written a poem on a subject of our choice. I wondered if Mrs. Higby could write a poem on the subject of her choice if somebody told her to do it. Probably not. It didn't seem to me like there was diddly-squat's worth of poetry in her anywhere. It was like she had this idea that kids were supposed to be creative, not her. To make it more embarrassing, each of us was supposed to recite our poem aloud, because "recitation is a language art too."

She went around the room calling on people. A

few kids got up and said really bad poems to tell her what they thought of the assignment. A lot of kids hadn't done it at all, which made her annoyed with everybody in general. Walking past Chav, she snipped at him. "We don't suppose *you* have anything," even though there was no way he should have.

But Chav stood up.

Maybe he did it to show her wrong. Maybe he did it to surprise everyone—which it did, it surprised us plenty. But I think he had deeper reasons, like there was something in him crying to be said.

Without speaking he went to the center of the front of the room. Everybody stared at him, including Mrs. Higby—especially Mrs. Higby—but he didn't look at any of us. I don't know where he was looking. Far away somewhere.

As though he had just that moment thought of it, he said:

> "*My life is made of midnight.*
> *The black horse of anger gallops closer.*
> *The moon in my sky is the color of death.*
> *The stars are chips of broken glass*
> *In a black back alley at midnight*
> *And the stallion gallops in my chest,*
> *The black horse of anger gallops.*
> *The world will die under his iron tread,*
> *And the moon in my sky is a cold dead eye*
> *At midnight.*"

4

His voice was low, but everybody heard every word, we were so quiet. Something about him stunned us.

Mrs. Higby's throat was jerking again. She said, "Very nice, Chav," without meaning it. It made sense that she wouldn't appreciate real poetry from a kid.

Chav didn't look at her as he sat down. He did not care about her approval or disapproval or the way everybody was goggling at him. Me too, and my mind was going like a hamster in an exercise wheel. Who was he? Where was he from? Was he older than the rest of us? He wasn't big, but in ways he seemed a lot older. That rugged face of his. The way he owned space when he was in it, instead of just borrowing it for a minute.

Mrs. Higby looked around the room and picked on me next, maybe because the horse in Chav's poem made her think of me, because she knew I liked horses. "Grace. You have a poem to share with us?"

I hate my name, because I'm not graceful and I'm tired of Amazing Grace jokes. My friends and family call me Gray, because I've got them trained, but Mrs. Higby wasn't trainable. I had tried.

"Grace Calderone." As if there were another Grace in there. "Your poem, please."

I shook my head. I had written something, but after Chav's poem it would have sounded stupid. It was about the fat little mare I rode sometimes. Her name was Paradiddle, she had funny hair that was curly all over, her legs were so short she trotted like a caterpillar, and she was the sweetest thing. I adored her. Yet in a way I didn't want to ride a ponyish horse like her. I'm a dreamer, and Chav's angry black stallion poem had pushed all my dream buttons. I didn't want to talk about my fuzzy little Paradiddle in front of him.

So I shook my head. "Grace, we're disappointed," Mrs. Higby grumped. "We were counting on you."

"But she does have something!" yelled out my best friend, Minda, who never knows when to keep her mouth shut. "I saw it, she showed it to me!" I turned around and glared at her, but she didn't shut up. "Come on, Gray, it's good!"

"Grace, recite your poem," Mrs. Higby ordered, so I had to. I didn't look at Chav, but once I was up there I decided to give it my best shot.

> *"She has curly hair—*
> *No, she's not a poodle.*
> *She's pudgy in the middle—*
> *No, she's not a teddy bear.*
> *She's a little brown mare,*
> *Her name is Paradiddle,*
> *And I can ride her*
> *Anywhere.*
> *So I look stupid, who cares?*
> *Laugh if you dare.*
> *Just bring me a saddle,*
> *Hand me a bridle.*

She's not a caterpillar,
She's a horse, so there!"

I hammed it up, and threw in a pout at the end. Most of the kids laughed and clapped. It was kind of nice that they liked my poem, and kind of awful, because who cared about them—what did the new boy think? Did Chav think I was a big overgrown jerk?

Finally I dared a look at him. He wasn't laughing. He was looking straight back at me, but I couldn't tell what he was thinking. His eyes were like black ice. I couldn't see into him at all.

※ ※ ※

At lunch he came through the line late and used one of those purple vouchers they give you at the office if you've forgotten your lunch money. Then he sat by himself to eat.

"Wake up, Gray," Minda teased me. She waved her hand in front of my face. I just shoved it away. Like I was the only person watching Chav and wondering about him? I wasn't. Half the school was trying to figure him out, because he was different. He acted different, and he talked differently than us. Not that he had an accent, exactly, or at least not any accent I knew. He just sounded different.

"*Gray* likes the *new* boy," Minda sang.

"Shut up!" I whacked at her. She ducked.

"Gray likes—"

This time when I whacked at her she put her arm in her plate getting away. Lunch was some sort of prechewed meat with canned gravy like pureed monkey brains. Truly gross. It latched onto Minda's sweater sleeve like alien slime. She screamed, "Ewwwww! Sick," but then at least she was too busy cleaning herself up to bother me. I sat and watched Chav some more. It wasn't true, what Minda was saying. I mean, I felt something for Chav but not what she meant. But she would never understand that. Probably nobody ever would.

Another different thing about Chav: he sat there eating his school lunch from one end to the other as if it were real food.

I wasn't the only one who noticed. Matt Kain, also known as Kain the Pain, got up and went over to hassle him.

"Hey, weenie! You hungry or something?"

Chav just looked up at him and kept eating.

"Hey!" Matt yelled to whoever would listen. "Look at this new dude! He eats cafeteria slop."

A couple of Matt's buddies grinned and yelled stuff back, but Chav didn't bother to say anything to any of them. He just kept eating.

Matt leaned over him and yelled like he was deaf, "Weirdo, you stupid? That crap ain't food. Don't you know dog barf when you see it?"

Chav kept eating. I got up, pretending to take

my tray back, and headed toward Kain the No-Brain Pain to tell him to let Chav alone.

"You'd eat manure, wouldn't you?" Matt was saying to Chav as I got close, and he stuck one big hand under Chav's plate to tip it up. Right then I saw that Chav didn't need any help from me, because the next instant Matt was wearing the whole tray, and Chav was on his feet with black fire in his eyes. Matt yelled a name I can't repeat and jumped at Chav to punch him out. And Matt was about three inches taller than Chav, and a lot huskier. But Chav met him like a head-on collision, and the next second Matt was staggering back—no wonder. The look on Chav's face even scared me, and I wasn't the one getting hit by him like getting kicked by a horse. Chav really knew what he was doing. Matt would have been flattened except a couple of his football buddies jumped up and grabbed Chav to stop the fight.

He let them hold him by the arms and barely seemed to notice them. But he spoke to Matt. "Listen, butthead," he said, "just let me alone."

"Like hell I will. I'm going to get you for this." With blood on his face and pukey canned gravy globbed all over the rest of him, Matt looked like he meant it. Sounded like he meant it too.

But Chav laughed. Not a TV bad-guy laugh, not a pose, but a real laugh as if something was actually funny, kind of. "Don't bother," he said in a matter-of-fact way. "I really don't care."

9

Then he pulled away from the guys who were holding him and walked off with not a spot of mess anywhere on those black clothes of his.

"Hot *dog*," somebody said. I came to and found that Minda was standing beside me. Lots of kids were gathered around—but no teachers, lucky for Chav and Matt. Parents think teachers are always playing cop at school, but they're not. In between classes teachers mostly don't want to be bothered.

"Holy crud," somebody else said. "Who the walk-on-water does he think he is?"

At the time I thought it was a stupid put-down. But it turned out to be the first question I should have asked about Chav and didn't. Who did he *think* he was?

Who was he?

* * *

"So what's new at school?" Liana asked me at supper. She's my aunt, but I never call her Aunt because it makes her seem old, which she's not. She's young and pretty and a pretty decent person to live with. When I was little I used to spell her name Lee Anna on Christmas tags and thank-you notes and things, because that was the way it sounded to me, and she never corrected me. That was the kind of person she was—people's feelings mattered to her, even if the person was just a little kid. Especially if it was just a little kid. She loved kids.

10

Supper was her homemade bacon-and-broccoli four-cheese thick-crust pizza, which is great. I was interested in eating, not talking about school. "Nothing," I said with my mouth full.

But Liana really wanted to talk, because she gets lonely being by herself most of the day. "Gray, give me a break. There has to be something. What was the best thing that happened to you today?"

"Chav." It was okay to say this, because Liana wouldn't tease.

"Chav? Is that a boy's name?" But she was cool, she didn't even smile the wrong way. Liana was hardly ever a pain—she was just kind of sad a lot, like living was a duty and an obligation and taking care of me was a responsibility. Those were words she used a lot, but she hardly ever said "enjoy." I missed my parents and brother probably as much as she missed her husband and kids, but I'd made up my mind to get over it. I had a life, and I don't think Liana really did. She just sort of watched mine, like watching TV.

"Yeah, he's a boy. He's new."

"See, I knew something was new." That was about as close as she ever got to teasing. And her smile almost brightened up her eyes. "What's he like?"

"Different."

"Different?"

"He doesn't talk like us and he doesn't dress like us and he's not friendly."

11

"Cute?"

"No, not really."

"But there's something about him?"

Sometimes she understood things too damn well. I chomped a big mouthful of pizza and didn't answer.

After a while she asked, "What was the worst thing that happened today?"

"The fight."

"You got into a fight with somebody?" This was not unknown to happen.

"No. Chav did."

"Oh. Was it bad?"

"Nobody got hurt or anything, but it was scary." Liana was looking at me kind of hard. "Why?"

But I just chewed pizza and shook my head and couldn't answer. Or wouldn't.

It wasn't that I was afraid of Chav himself, exactly. But I was starting to understand about the black stallion of anger galloping in his chest. It was his heart, and it frightened me. The rage in him might trample anybody, even a girl.

CHAPTER

— 2 —

Journal   *Mrs. Higby*
Oct. 15   *Language Arts*
Chav

Journal
Oct. 15
Chav

We are supposed to keep a journal ten minutes every day in this class. I don't know what to say. If I could talk or sing instead of having to write, I would do better.

Nobody is supposed to look at this journal. But why would the teacher make us write it if she is not going to look at it? MRS. HIGBY, YOU ARE A WART ON THE TUSH OF THE WORLD. If she looks at this and has a heart attack, it will be her own fault for being a lying gadjo.

There is one person here I like, a girl who has a feeling about horses. But she is a gadjo too. Never trust a gadjo. That was my mother's mistake. I will not make friends with any gadjos. I do not want any friends. What is the point? In a few weeks I will be someplace else. It is a big country. I am not likely to run out of places before I run out of time.

The gadjo girl is not very pretty anyway. She is tall and pale and has a big nose and big legs like two-by-fours.

I do not believe I let Baval and Chavali talk me into this going to school. But they are right, the school is warm at least, and it is easy to get something to eat. In a way they are right, that if I am going to make them go, I ought to go myself. But in a way they are wrong, because they do not understand: they are going to grow up and have families and be happy, but I am not. They are going to need education, but I am not. Once they are big enough to take care of themselves, then they will not need me anymore, and that will be it for Chav. I will steal a gun and go to a country club or somewhere and take with me as many gadjos as I can before I dispose of myself.

Time's up.

*　　*　　*

14

> *Gray Calderone*
> *Ride a black horse*
> *Ride a high wind*
> *Tame a black stallion*
> *Tame the wind*
> *Tame the thunderstorm*
> *Gentle the wind*
> *Make it your friend*
> *Gentle the wind*

After the first couple of days I started to catch on that Chav was poor. I heard he borrowed soap and shampoo in gym class. I noticed he wore the exact same clothes both days, and he didn't bring lunch money the second day, either. And he ate every bit of his lunch again even though it was cafeteria macaroni and cheese, which is like stinky puke-yellow rubber. This time there were teachers around—I guess the custodian reported the mess on the floor—so Matt Kain didn't do anything except look ugly at him and yell a few things. Chav didn't bother to look up or yell back.

The next morning I packed lunch. A lot of lunch, just in case.

I left the house real early, before Liana was awake, because she is depressing to be around in the morning. She takes pills to sleep, and then waking up hits her like a club. Sometimes she cries. I could go stay with my grandparents, who are actually my legal guardians according to my parents' will, but I keep sticking it out with Liana. We're really close. She was with me when it happened; we hung onto each other all through that first awful night, and we've been together ever since. We each know what the other has been through like nobody else does. Anyway, Grandpa is a cop, and Grandma is a teacher, a good one— there are some good ones—but the point is they're both paranoid, always asking if I'm okay, do I want to talk about anything, and looking into my eyes like they're checking for drugs. Liana isn't like that. She trusts me.

It was a terrific day. Indian summer. The way the sun hit the orange and yellow trees they were blazing like fire. I walked to school real slow, scuffing through the leaves on the ground, and I took the long way around, through the fields behind the elementary school and into the beech grove at the bottom of the nature trail. It's like a hollow down there, hidden from everything, peaceful. I walked deep into the woods.

All this is to explain that I wasn't trying to spy on Chav. It just happened that I saw him.

I saw him riding a black horse between the golden trees.

I don't know which I saw first, the horse or Chav. It was like they were both part of the same king-crowned-in-gold thing, the black stallion—I could tell it was a stallion by its thick arched neck—the black horse treading through the fiery leaves and the black-haired boy on its back. The horse was small and slim, like Chav, and it carried its head high like him. It curved its neck and struck out with its forefeet like a dancer as it walked. Its head was long and Roman-nosed, not pretty at all—it was way better than pretty, it was fierce and proud. This horse was a real black, with not a white or a brown hair on it anywhere, so black it seemed awesome, packed with itself, like it was more of a horse than other horses. And it was headed toward me.

It would have been lucky-day amazing to see a horse, any sort of horse, on my way to school when I wasn't expecting it, but a black stallion yet! I couldn't believe it. I stood there hugging a tree trunk and gawking so hard I didn't see the other two kids at first. They were on the horse too, a little girl in front of Chav and a not-so-little boy behind him, all three of them riding bareback to school as if this black stallion were a tired old mare, with just a halter and a couple of rope reins.

Then Chav glanced over toward me, his face changed, and his whole body went stiff. The black horse stopped in its tracks that minute, before he even touched the rope reins. I knew it had to be because the change in his seat had signaled for a halt, but how many horses will respond that way? It was eerie, almost like he and the black horse were sharing a mind.

From about ten feet away they were staring at

me, and I realized from the spooked look in their eyes that neither of them had known I was there, or they probably wouldn't have come anywhere near me. The little girl riding in front of Chav twisted around and hid her face against his chest, shy or scared. All I could see was her long dark hair. The not-so-little boy looked at me with wide dark eyes from behind Chav's shoulder.

"Hi," I whispered, and I unlatched myself from my tree and walked a few steps toward them, slowly, trying not to startle the horse. "Hello, wild horse," I said softly to the stallion, taking a guess that it was some kind of mustang. I wanted to make friends with it. "What's his name?" I asked.

He looked stone-faced but answered me. "Rom."

"Huh?" It didn't seem like enough name for such a horse.

"Rom."

I realized I reminded me of somebody. "Spell it," I said, straight-faced. "We beg your pardon? What is his last name? We need his last name for the records."

That cracked Chav's stony face open. He actually laughed, a happier laugh than the one he'd given Matt Kain. The way he laughed made the little kids decide everything was all right. The little girl squirmed around and looked at me—her face was petal-smooth and pretty, like a brown flower—I wished I was half as pretty. The boy behind Chav slipped down off the horse and grinned at me as soon as his beat-up sneakers hit the ground. "I'm Baval," he announced like it was important, "and this is Chavali." He helped the little girl down. When she stuck her feet out I noticed her sneakers looked real old, like Baval's, yet they were too big for her, and she didn't have socks on. "Say hi," Baval told her once she was down, but she didn't. She smiled at me, then got shy again and ducked her head against Baval. They both wore blue jeans and T-shirts, plenty old and worn out, but still Baval and Chavali seemed basically like regular kids. Their strange names and dark skins made them different than me and my friends but not as different as Chav. Their faces were soft and young, not flinty like his. Their eyes were clear and sunny, not hard like black ice. Something about him was a lot more different.

"I'm Gray," I told Chavali and Baval. "Hi. Do you always ride Rom to school?"

They looked at each other and kind of smiled, but nobody answered. Chav did not even look up. He was down off Rom and had the halter off him and was crouching in front of him, using the rope reins to loop hobbles around his forelegs. Rom put his head down and nuzzled Chav's hair, and Chav did not push his big black nose away.

"Hi, Rom," I said to the stallion. He swung his head up and looked at me with deep, wise eyes, and I knew he would allow me to pat him, though I meant nothing to him. I went over and stroked his

19

neck. There were some scars on his back and shoulders, which was a rotten shame, but none of them seemed fresh. His coat was smooth and shiny. Somebody had been taking good care of him.

Chav got the rope hobbles adjusted just right and stood up so that all of a sudden he was facing me. "Do people come down here?" he asked. "Will anybody find him here?"

I couldn't answer for a minute, because the question meant so many things. It meant that for some reason—I didn't want to think what reason—Rom was not supposed to be found. It meant that I was not "people," not just anybody, but someone who knew a secret. It meant I could not tell. Chav wanted me on his side, even though I was not sure who the sides were or what they were fighting over. He trusted me not to tell.

He was right. I wouldn't.

"Nobody much comes down here during the week," I said finally. New rules: Science teachers were supposed to keep kids up top because kids kept getting "lost" down in the hollow. "But people hike here weekends, and they'll find the hoofprints and horse piles and stuff."

Chav shrugged as if the weekend were so far away only an idiot would think about it. He looked at Baval and Chavali, and without another word all three of them walked off.

"Wait," I called, and I tossed my paper sack at them. Chav caught it.

"What's this?" he asked.

"Lunch."

He stared at me.

"Take it," I told him, and I headed toward my school, the middle school, which was across campus from the elementary school. Probably Baval and Chavali were going there. I didn't look back to make sure, because Chav was behind me in the hollow somewhere, and he was more like a wild horse than the black horse was. Like a spooked colt. I had to be careful not to scare him.

I saw him in language arts, but he didn't look at me, so I didn't say anything to him.

I didn't tell anyone, not even Minda, but all day I thought of the black stallion not far away, moving softly through the woods, eating the golden leaves.

At lunchtime Chav borrowed money from a teacher and bought himself a barfburger. What had he done with the lunch I gave him? Gave it to Baval and Chavali, maybe?

Who was he? Where did he come from? Where did he live?

"Earth to Gray," Minda teased me as I watched him. She was sharing her lunch with me, but I wasn't talking. "Earth to Gray. Is there life on your planet?"

I shook my head.

"None at all?"

"Nope." I wasn't about to tell her what was going on inside my head.

Sitting there thinking, I had made up my mind what I was going to do.

❋   ❋   ❋

Just because it was such a beautiful day, Liana knew I would want to go to the stable right after school. So there she was in the car waiting for me, and she'd brought along a pack of Twinkies for me and a carrot for Paradiddle.

"Way to go, Lee!" I called her that sometimes.

"What's new in school?" she asked me.

"Nothing, really." I got out of my shoes and into my riding boots while she drove. Other than that, I didn't have to change anything. I wore the same jeans to school and to ride. Liana didn't mind when they got stained with horse sweat—we would just go out and buy more. I'll say one thing for horrible accidents: between Uncle Dan's life insurance and my parents' life insurance and the money from my parents' house and stuff, we didn't have to worry about getting by. I mean, we weren't millionaires, but we had enough.

That's the only thing I'll say for horrible accidents, though. Believe me, it was not the best way to get money.

So anyway Lee drove me out to the stable, which was really more like a farm, not a fancy place where people wore breeches and schooled for shows. Those places are okay, I guess, but I like Topher the Gopher's stable better. There was a wooden sign up, Agony Acres, but that was just one of Topher's lame jokes. Nobody really called it that—everybody who rode there just called it the stable. It was just a sort of down-home place in the country, and he was just a sort of sandy-haired guy who loved horses. His wife had left him because she was jealous of the way he loved horses—she wanted him to work a job with regular hours or something. She was named Chris, short for Christina, which was why people called him Topher, because his name was Christopher and it would have been confusing to call him Chris too.

"Why didn't she just change her name to Tina?" I asked him once.

"She didn't like it."

"But you like the name Topher?"

"Not really." But he grinned. "I got to admit it's different." He drawled a little when he talked because he came from Texas or someplace, and he always wore his cowboy hat and boots even though he rode English, and he knew dressage, but he taught all his horses to ground-tie like cow ponies. I liked him a lot.

Now he didn't want to be called Chris anymore because it reminded him of Christina. And he didn't have a wife anymore, but he still had horses, all kinds. He had Arabs, Appaloosas, a big old Belgian mare, a Paso Fino, a white Thoroughbred filly off the track with a blown tendon, a dapple-gray Connemara, Tennessee walkers, quarter horses, and of course Paradiddle, who seemed to be at least part Bashkir Curly. He'd got her at an auction when she was a foal, and, surprise, when she grew up she had curly hair.

Paradiddle's name, by the way, means a certain kind of drumbeat. Kind of like the way her hooves sound when she's trying to keep up with horses that have actual legs instead of caterpillar appendages.

"Hi, Topher!" I yelled as soon as I got out of the car, because there he was, leaning on a paddock fence and looking at his new Thoroughbred to see if the tendon was getting any better. "Can I take Paradiddle out for a long ride?"

"Sure." Most of the time Topher saved Paradiddle for me, I guess because he could see we got along. If other people came to ride, he put them on the quarter horses, which were more like what people expected, horsewise. "Is Minda coming? I'll get Dude." Dude was the pretty palomino-and-white pinto Minda usually rode.

"Not today." She had a dentist appointment. Usually I liked to ride with Minda, but today I had a plan that didn't include her.

Liana handed a check out the car window for me to give to Topher. She hardly ever got out of the car at the stable. No reason why. She just didn't. There were a lot of fun things Lee didn't do.

"Don't worry if I'm late," I told her. I had

maybe four hours before dark. It was still daylight saving time for another week or two.

"Okay. Have a good ride. Call me when you need to be picked up." She drove off.

Topher didn't have to help me do anything. The check was a rental fee because he owned Diddle and fed her and took care of her. He wasn't a gofer really—he had taught me to ride, but now I was on my own. I went down to the pasture and caught Diddle myself, and gave her her carrot and told her what a pretty girl she was, and led her up to the barn. But Topher hung around while I curried her and brushed her, because he was a friend.

"How's stuff?" I asked him.

"Better." That was what he always said, "better." Better than what?

"How's Red?" That was the white Thoroughbred filly. He called her Red because Thoroughbreds aren't supposed to be white. Topher had a strange sense of humor.

"Better. Gonna be fine, just needs a good long rest. By spring that tendon ought to be sound again. Then I can think about retraining her."

"Can I help?"

"Sure."

Out of nowhere I said, "I wish I had a horse of my own."

I guess Topher was used to hearing this. He just said, "You sort of do," and nodded at Diddle, who was standing there with her big blimpy belly stick-

25

ing out and her big blinky eyes half closed and her brown curly forelock hanging down over them.

"Oh, poor Diddle." I kissed her on her fuzzy forehead. "Don't listen to me." I combed the poodle curls of her mane like my life depended on it, but I said to Topher, "I think Liana might get me a horse for Christmas."

This was true. We had enough money, so she had promised she was going to get me my own horse sometime soon. And Christmas was coming.

"Think so? What kind?"

"I don't care. Any kind or color is fine with me as long as it's a real horse."

"Real?"

"You know, big and strong and fast. Like—you know. Didn't you ever want a black stallion or something?"

He smiled, and I guess he sort of understood, because he said, "I want them all."

Ten minutes later I was riding Diddle across the fields, and she trotted along like a big dog, and her fuzzy little brown ears were tilted forward happily as always. She was such a good horse. But I was thinking about a black stallion and the boy who rode it.

CHAPTER

—— 3 ——

It took me an hour to get to the school. I had never ridden there before—why would I? It wasn't as if I didn't spend enough time there already. And the roads went the long way around, and paved roads aren't the best place to ride horseback anyhow, because of stupid people in cars, among other reasons. So I had to find ways through woods and housing developments and cow pastures with barbed-wire fences. It was sort of challenging.

When I finally got to the hollow where the black stallion had spent the day, he was gone, of course. I was expecting that.

"Okay, Diddle, here we go," I told her, and I guided her along where I could see scuffed-up leaves. We were going to try to follow the black stallion's trail.

At first it was easy. The cornfields below the

27

hollow were marshy from runoff, and I could see the black horse's hoofprints between the stubble. I could even tell that he wasn't shod. But after that it got harder. We came to an overgrown field, and all I had to go by was a faint whitish line in the grass and weeds where he had passed through. Then on the far side was a gravel road. I could only guess which direction the black horse had gone on that, and I spent maybe half an hour riding around in circles. Any other horse would have thrown a fit, but Diddle didn't mind.

This was taking a lot of time. "We should head back," I told her.

But we didn't, because finally I found a mark in the mud and weeds alongside the road that might have been a hoofprint—I wasn't sure. So I went farther and, all riiiight! I found the trail again in a farmer's dirt lane. Then I lost it in a clover field. . . . I could spend an hour telling how I kept losing those hoofprints and finding them again, going across the fields to the railroad track, then along the track to—

The trestle?

"You have to be kidding," I begged. But Chav and the black stallion were not kidding. I could see the oval-shaped depressions in the gravel between the ties, going straight across, sixty feet above the deep part of the river, on a narrow bridge with no side rails. At least this railroad bridge was solid, made of steel and concrete—it was not the spindly kind of trestle that was full of holes. But even so, what if a train came? What if the horse acted up? What if a bird flew across in front of Diddle's nose and she spooked? I could end up in the—water—and to make it worse, I was scared of water ever since . . . ever since a couple of years before. Water was a back stabber to me. On the surface it twinkled and sparkled and smiled, but underneath, it was drowning deep.

"Oopsie, it's really getting late," I told the world. "Time to go home." But I didn't go. I hated being scared and I didn't like to give in to it. Maybe it was okay to be scared, maybe it was even reasonable under the circumstances, but something in me wasn't being reasonable about this Chav-and-Rom thing.

If they could do it . . .

There Diddle stood with her ears sideward, swishing her curly tail and waiting for me to make up my mind. If any horse in the world could take me safely across that bridge, Diddle could. All of a sudden I was mad—at myself, mostly, for being a back stabber about Diddle. No black stallion was better than her.

"Okay, girl, let's do it." I listened hard—no train was coming. Then I sent her forward.

She nodded along, stepping between the ties, never even looking at the river glinting too far below. What a trail horse she was. The best. I let her handle it and sat tight and tried not to look down. In a way it was nothing.

And in a way it was the most important thing I

had ever done, because on the other side were Chav and the black horse.

At the corner where the railroad and the river met, screened off by trees, with nothing around it but woods, was an abandoned farm. I saw the top of the yellow brick silo first, with the low sun hitting it and turning it gold. In the shadows were the falling-down barn and farmhouse. Then I saw the black stallion grazing where the sun hit the top of the meadow, and I stopped Diddle on the tracks because my breath had stopped. There were no fence, no hobbles, no halter line. The grazing stallion was as free as a wild thing, and lying on its back like he was asleep, like being rocked in a black-horse cradle, with his face in its mane and his arms down around its shoulders, was Chav. He had his shirt off, and the heat of the horse and the sunshine were keeping him warm. His bare skin pressed against the horse's skin. His black hair hung down and mixed with the black horse's mane. He had his eyes closed; he didn't see me.

Together the two of them were so beautiful that when I breathed in, it was like a sob. Now it felt all wrong for me to be there. Why was I being so none-of-my-business nosy, following him? I would have turned Diddle around and gone home that minute—but right then a high, happy voice yelled, "Hey! It's her!" and there were Baval and Chavali.

They came running up from the silo. "Come see

our castle," Baval called as if I were an old friend, so I rode down the meadow to meet them. They both stood and watched Diddle with wide eyes.

"What kind of horse is that?" Baval wanted to know.

"Fat and furry."

"No, I mean—did you give her a perm all over?"

"Can I ride her?" Chavali asked, which took a lot when she was so shy, and of course I got off Diddle and lifted her on. I led Diddle, and Chavali rode, and Baval ran ahead down to the castle, which turned out to be the silo. With its big bricks sticking up jagged at the top where its roof had come off, it did look sort of like a castle tower. At the bottom somebody had knocked loose an archway of bricks, enough so that a kid could crawl in, and there were blankets and things in there, and a tarp covering the ground, and another one rigged up overhead.

"Are you camping out here or something?" I asked Baval. It seemed strange. Where were the adults? Did these kids have parents who let them do this? The days were still warm enough, but the nights were getting cold.

He giggled and didn't answer. Then I heard footsteps and turned around, and there was Chav.

He wasn't looking at me, just at Diddle, but I looked at him. There were scars on his chest and shoulders, and I realized the leatheriness of his face was probably scarring too. Now, looking back,

I can't believe I didn't see right away: somebody had done terrible things to him. But then it never occurred to me, because in my family no adult did bad things to little kids. Nobody had ever hit me except other kids. I just figured Chav must have been in a horrible accident, maybe a fire, and probably he didn't want to talk about it, because I knew I didn't want to talk about the accident that had killed my mother and father and brother.

"So this is the mare with curly hair," Chav said, touching Diddle, rubbing the itchy place in the middle of her forehead. "Are you sure she's not a poodle?"

"She's a good trail horse."

"Or a dachshund? Could she be part dachshund? Her legs are short enough." But he was patting Diddle the whole time. He really liked her, I could tell, and I started to like him.

"Down," Chavali ordered, holding out her arms to him.

"She's your sister, right?" I asked him as he swung her off Diddle.

"Yes."

"And Baval is your brother."

He nodded, and then he picked up his shirt from the ground and put it on, and then since he seemed to be in a mellow mood I asked him right out, "Did you guys run away from home or what?"

He looked straight at me for the first time, and in a strange, intense way he said, "We are of the ancient tribe of Romany. Home is where our heads lie. We do not run away from anything. We wander in search of our king."

"Tell her, Chav!" Baval said eagerly. "Tell her about us."

"Tell *us*, Chav!" That was Chavali. She hung on to his leg. Baval grabbed him around the waist.

"Tell Gray!" Baval begged.

"Supper first," Chav said.

He made a fire in front of the "castle," and I took off Diddle's bridle and saddle and let her graze with Rom. Then we sat around the fire to be warm and eat. Supper turned out to be the lunch I had given them—some Fritos, a few carrot sticks, and two peanut-butter-and-jelly sandwiches for four people. Make that three people, because I didn't take any. My stomach was growling like a chained-up dog, but I said I had to wait, my aunt would be expecting me to eat with her. Chav didn't eat either, until little Chavali said she was done. Then he finished the corner of a sandwich she had left.

"Tell Gray," Baval insisted. He looked like he was about ten years old, maybe even twelve, but he acted younger. When Chavali went over to Chav and sat on his lap, Baval had to cuddle up against him too.

"Okay." With the little kids piled on top of him, Chav leaned back against the wall of the silo. He looked at me but past me, into the distance.

Softly, as if starting a conversation, he said, "Our mother was a princess of Romany, a daughter of a king of Romany. Our father was a prince of the Rom. He was tall. He had real Andalusian horses and they would not let a stranger touch them, but they would come when he called them. He had black hair and true blue eyes and he wore a head-band made out of gold coins and he loved to dance."

"And play guitar," Baval put in.

"Right."

"And he had gentle hands," said Chavali anxiously.

"Yes. Gentle hands."

Something strange was going on. I knew their mother wasn't a princess or their father a prince, any more than I was a rock star. It just didn't feel true. I knew this story of Chav's was all a whooping lie, and he knew I knew—the slantwise way he looked at me told me that. But he didn't care what I thought, because he was giving the story to Baval and Chavali. And they seemed to need it. They believed every word he told them.

"Our father loved our mother because she was very beautiful," he said, kind of singsong. "But a bad gadjo man kidnapped us and our mother." Gadjo? What kind of bad guy was that? "He took us away from our Romany tribe and kept us prisoner." Chav was not looking at me or at the little kids but off into the darkening meadow where the black horse was grazing. "He called himself our father, but we know our real father is a prince of the Rom, because our mother told us so. When she was dying, when she was lying in a white lace bed with her long hair streaming down and her face very pale like an angel's, she hugged me and whispered in my ear and told me we must go find our real father."

"She gave you a kiss," Chavali said.

"Yes." Chav swallowed. "She gave me a kiss and she gave me this." He pulled something out of his jeans pocket and held it in the cup of his hand—Baval and Chavali both touched it, and their soft young faces in the firelight looked like the faces of people in church. "Our father will have more like it, and that's how we will know him." Chav put it away again. "For years the king of Romany and the prince of Romany have been wandering and searching for us. Now we are searching for them. Someday we will meet at a crossroad."

"And our real father will be glad to see us?" Baval asked.

"He will be so glad he will order a truckload of pizza and have a feast and let us ride his horses and give us his headband to wear."

"And he will keep us?" Chavali asked anxiously. "And he will not let the gadjo man take us away anymore?"

"Yes." Chav looked tired. He lifted her off his lap. "Bedtime."

Because of the fire and the story I hadn't realized how dark it was getting. The sky was gray,
almost black, only streaked with orange a little bit
toward one edge. "Holy crud," I yipped, and I
jumped up and ran to catch Paradiddle, get the
saddle and bridle back on her, and start home
while there was still a little light left.

Chav left the little kids at the silo and followed
me without saying anything. He helped me tack
up, and I noticed he knew what he was doing.

"What does gadjo mean?" I asked while we got
Diddle ready.

"You are a gadjo." I could not see his face, but I
could hear the hardness in his voice like a challenge. "You are not Rom."

I didn't have time to hang around and talk
about it, or tell him what I was sure he already
knew, that the thing his mother was supposed to
have given him was nothing but a fake plastic gold
dollar from some kid's set of play money.

His voice still hard, he asked, "Are you going to
tell people about us?"

I shot back, "Why should I?" And I got on
Paradiddle and got moving. As I rode out, the
black stallion was a darker place in the darkness
of the night with his head up, watching.

Paradiddle was an angel horse as usual and got
me back to the stable okay, even in the dark. We
didn't have to go over the railroad trestle again,
or back to the school. All we had to do was follow

the tracks the other way awhile, then cut cross country to the stable.

Topher had all the floodlights on and was waiting for me. He didn't say anything until I got off Paradiddle, and then all he said was, "Your aunt's been calling. She's worried."

"I went on the other side of the tracks, and then there was a train, and it stopped, and I had to wait for it to get out of the way." This was partly true. Chav's camp was on the other side of the tracks. There had been a train while we were eating.

Topher said, "So was I. Worried."

That surprised me. I didn't know what to say.

"Go call your aunt," he told me. "I'll take care of Diddle."

So I did what he said, I went to the barn phone and called Liana, and it was okay. I told her the same thing I told Topher, and she was cool. One reason she lets me go horseback riding is that people told her the accident would make her overprotective of me, and she doesn't want to be that way. So sometimes she goes pretty far in the other direction. I think she would let me try out for football if I wanted to.

While I was waiting for her to come pick me up I helped Topher give the horses their grain. "Sorry I worried you," I said.

"That's okay."

"Do you know what Romany is?" I asked him. "Or Rom?"

He gave me a blank look. "Come again?"

"Romany. Do you know what the people of Romany are?"

"Beats me. Where'd you hear about them?"

I spilled feed so I wouldn't have to answer.

CHAPTER

4

"They're Gypsies," Peck the blacksmith was saying to Topher. I had just walked into the stable, but somehow I knew right away he was talking about Chav and Baval and Chavali. "Thieving Gypsies. They can call themselves what they like, I know a Gypsy when I see one." He sounded angry. His big arms bulged with muscle as he banged a shoe onto a quarter horse named Termite because it chewed on wood. "Them dark faces and sly eyes. They can't fool me. You better lock everything up, Worthwine." That was Topher's last name. Peck's last name was Fischel, and besides being the horseshoer he was the farmer next door. "You better tie down what you can't hide. They'll steal the weathercock off the barn if you ain't careful."

"I ain't missing anything," Topher said quietly.

"Who?" Minda demanded. "Who steals?" She

had just walked in. It was Saturday, and we were going to go for our Saturday ride.

"Them Gypsies," Peck said without even looking up. "Camping in the old Altland place. You can see their fire if you walk out along the tracks."

"Coolness!"

I didn't agree with Minda. To me it felt more like hot water–ness. It was a good thing Mr. Fischel was bent over a horse's foot and not looking at me, because I'm sure my face looked scared, and I was leaning against a wall and sort of hanging on, hoping Minda wouldn't guess we were talking about Chav. I hadn't told her anything about the black stallion or the kids living in the silo or anything. I hadn't told anyone.

"I just seen a few of the kids so far," Peck said, "but where there's a few there's always a passel of them. No-goods." He growled, "Somebody ought to call young Altland and tell him to get his butt out there and run them off."

Topher had his back to me, holding the horse while Peck shoed it, so I couldn't see his face. But his voice sounded careful-quiet as he said, "It always seemed to me if Gypsies stole everything people blame them for, they'd need moving vans to haul it around."

Mr. Fischel straightened up and looked at him. "They thieve," he said kind of hard. "Take my word for it."

Minda's no rocket scientist in school, but she's smart about people. She knew it was time for us to slide on out of there or get caught in the cross fire. "Come on, Gray," she sang, and we went to catch Dude and Diddle and get them ready.

We didn't talk about Gypsies or anything while we groomed and tacked up. Mr. Fischel was still shoeing horses and we didn't want him to overhear. But once we were riding out across the fields Minda said, "You want to ride up the tracks and look at the Gypsies?"

"*No.*" It came out louder than I had meant it to. Minda looked over at me as Dude and Diddle walked along side by side. Then she said real gently, "It's Chav, isn't it?"

Like I said, she isn't stupid. And she is a good friend. "Maybe," I admitted. "I'm not sure." I knew there was no passel of Gypsies around Chav's camp. "Don't believe everything Peck said," I burst out. "He's ignorant."

She teased, "I'll tell him you said so."

"Right. Sure. You do that."

We couldn't really say anything to make Peck Fischel mad at us, because whenever we rode we crossed his land. Right now we were on his property, following his tractor path up his hill past the fenced-in Fischel cemetery that was supposed to be the oldest family burial plot in the county. Peck Fischel's people had been here for centuries, and he owned most of the land this side of the railroad.

41

From Chav's point of view he was a real gadjo, I guess.

And I guessed gadjo was a Gypsy word . . . but something felt wrong. Thinking about what Peck had said felt like listening to Chav's story about his mother's being a princess of Romany. There was some truth in it somewhere, but it would take a lot of getting to.

I said, "Why would a Gypsy kid go to school?"

"Yeah, anyway." Minda thought a minute. "But he hasn't been doing the work, Gray. It's like he's not expecting to stay."

That was the feeling I got too, yet I argued with her. "Lots of boys don't do their work."

"But he hasn't joined anything. He doesn't even say hi to anybody."

"It's too soon. Maybe he's shy."

Minda looked at me and didn't say anything. We rode awhile longer, past the cemetery. Then she asked, "Do you think Chav is a thief?"

Damn, she was good. Like a mind reader. How did she know what was bothering me, when she didn't even know about the black stallion? My mind kept backing up and backing up—I was telling myself there might have been a lot of reasons why Chav hid the horse down in the hollow during the day and nobody was supposed to know. Like probably horses weren't allowed on school property. Or he didn't want kids messing with Rom. He just wanted to keep the stallion to himself.

Or maybe Rom didn't belong to him at all.

What if he had stolen Rom? Wasn't that what Gypsies were supposed to do, steal horses? What if he stole horses from Topher? What if he stole Diddle?

If anything bad happened, it would be all my fault for not saying something.

Yet I didn't answer Minda's question. "Just ride," I told her.

"Want to gallop?"

Of course I did. "Noooooo. Who, me? Gallop?"

Minda just rose in her stirrups and leaned forward a little, and Dude ran. I had to kick Paradiddle. She galloped like a pig. Not that pigs can't go pretty fast. As we thundered along I yelled with happiness—yet I thought, I bet Rom gallops like the wind before a storm.

＊　　＊　　＊

Chav awoke from a dream of a giant fist hitting him, smashing him in the head, blood running down. He lay shaking and could not go back to sleep. The night was too cold. But maybe it was not just coldness keeping him awake. He ached as if he had really been beaten, and he had the strange feeling in his chest again, the one that would not let him lie still. Giving in to it, he tossed half of his blankets over Baval and the other half over Chavali, pulled on his shoes, and crawled out of the silo.

The night was as dark as his dream. He couldn't see a thing, but it felt good to stand up. He stretched, then shivered and hugged himself. Cold.

Partly it was the damn gadjo girl bothering him, he decided, the girl named, of all things, Gray. The minute she came here he should have packed up Baval and Chavali and moved on. He like her for the way she loved horses, but that was no excuse for him to take risks. What if she told somebody, what if authorities came and put him in jail? Or put him and Baval and Chavali in one of their horrible homes, just as bad as a jail? Or, worst of all, sent them back to their father? The gadjo girl had found out too much. He should have gotten out of there.

"I am of the ancient tribe of Romany," he told the night in jeering tones, mocking himself. "I do not run from anything."

What a joke. His mother was no princess—more like a slave. Dad practically wiped his feet on her. Whenever he said *do*, she did, and he had taken everything Gypsy away from her, even her language; she was not allowed to speak Romany or teach it to her children. Chav knew only a few words. That gadjo girl Gray could tell he was a big fake—he could see it in her eyes. She knew he would be running all his miserable life until he ended it. Her steady gaze saw through him. She knew too much.

"Jerk," Chav scolded himself. "Chicken." He jogged in place, then started walking up the meadow, trying to get warm. His numb feet stumbled on the uneven ground, and he couldn't see where he was going. The pressure in his chest was worse than ever.

Even if Gray wasn't a danger, it was time, past time. . . . He and his brother and sister should have been on a southbound freight by now, heading toward Florida or Texas or Georgia, someplace warm to spend the winter. That was what they had done last year, and it had worked okay. That was why he was here, along the tracks: to jump a freight. Trains passed every day. Some of them even stopped, for some inscrutable railroad reason. Yet he had not taken advantage of any of them.

Last year there hadn't been Rom.

In front of him the night seemed to gather itself into an even blacker blackness. Chav froze where he was—there was a shape coming at him, like in his bad dreams when the huge heavy pain struck him out of nowhere. But then he heard the soft clop of unshod hooves. "Rom," he whispered, and when the horse came up to him he threw his arms around the base of the stallion's neck and leaned against the warmth of Rom's shoulder.

After a few minutes the pressure in his chest eased up. Good. The one thing he absolutely positively swear-to-God did not want to do was blow up at Baval and Chavali. So far he had managed not to. For the year and a half they had been on their own he had not hit them or even screamed at them—unlike his darling father.

The anger started kicking inside Chav again. Someday it was going to bust him wide open, and then look out world.

He took a few deep breaths and tried to get his mind going. Some nights when he could not sleep he made up songs and poetry in his head. That was what he used to do when he was shut in the dark closet, make up stories and poems and songs. It was a way of staying real when the punishment was trying to make him smaller and smaller and less and less until he was nothing anymore, not a person at all.

He murmured to the horse one he had been working on:

> "My horse shines
> like a black neon sign
> in a black bar window
> on a black wet night
> so slick it's white.
> My horse moves
> like a black Harley cruising
> like black fire burning—"

Rom nuzzled his back.

Chav quit trying. His chest hurt. Words had

power, but they weren't helping this time. They couldn't help him leave Rom behind.

Rom was—Rom was a reason for living, and it was killing him.

"What am I going to do?" he whispered to the horse. "I got you away from that place, but now I can't take you with me. No way you can hop a freight."

❋   ❋   ❋

Minda had to visit her mother's grandmother in the nursing home the next day, and I asked to go riding. "Do you really have to?" Liana complained at me, which was about as close as she ever came to getting on my case. "I thought maybe we could do something together. Go to the mall or something." She wanted me to keep her company.

"Please," I begged, "the good weather will be gone soon."

That was true. But in a way it was a lie, because I was hiding things from her, such as the reason I really wanted to go, and the raisin packs and Snickers bars and cheese crackers and bologna sandwiches filling all my pockets. I felt guilty and miserable as she drove me out to the stable, but that didn't make me say anything.

Topher was just coming out of his house. When he saw the car pull in he called, "Hi, Gray," but then he walked over and said, "Hi, Mrs. Quinn, how's it going?" to my aunt, and he stood there

47

talking to her through the car window. This was not something he'd done before, but it's a free country. I went to catch Diddle, so I didn't hear what they were saying.

When I was grooming, Topher came into the barn and watched me.

"How's stuff?" I asked him.

"Better."

"Better than what?"

"Better than before. Gray, can I ask you something?"

"Sure." I stopped currying Diddle to look at him. He wasn't looking straight at me.

"If this is too personal, don't answer," he said. "I just wondered—somebody told me—your aunt lost her husband and kids in some kind of boating accident?"

So far this was not being a real good day. I felt myself go wooden inside like a taxidermy project, like I had been stuffed and mounted for public display, which is what always happens when somebody brings this up. But I made myself nod and say something. "My mother and father and brother too. Same accident."

"Oh, jeez, I'm sorry!" Topher said it like he meant it. "I—I didn't know you were involved."

I went back to currying Diddle. "I don't want to talk about it," I told Topher.

"That's okay. You don't have to. Dumb," he grumbled, tapping himself on the forehead. "Ever since the divorce I've been so busy feeling sorry for myself, I haven't been paying attention to anything."

At least he understood I couldn't discuss it. My grandmother and other people kept telling me I should try, I wouldn't really get over it until I could talk about it, but too bad. I just couldn't.

"Tell me just one thing," Topher said. "How long ago was it?"

"Two years." A little more now. The two-year anniversary, if you can call it that, had been in August. A couple of months before Chav showed up.

"It's really none of my business," Topher said softly, almost like he was talking to himself. "It's just that—up until recently I never got to know your aunt. We talked a lot that night you stayed out so damn late. She was upset, but she never raised her voice at me or tried to blame me the way a lot of parents would have done. Hell, she tried to keep *me* from worrying. She's really something."

That sounded like Liana. I nodded at Topher and kept making Diddle happy—she loved the feel of the rubber currycomb. Topher kept watching me. I guess he could tell I still felt kind of rocky, because then he went and got the saddle for me when he wouldn't have had to. "Listen," he said, "I'm sorry. It was a dumb thing to ask."

"Stop it with the sorries," I grumped at him. "You can ask me dumb things anytime you want to."

That was the truth. I liked Topher a lot. More

than I liked Chav, in a way, because liking Topher was simple and liking Chav was complicated. But in a way I liked Chav more, because being around him was like riding a black stallion.

CHAPTER

— 5 —

When I got to the deserted Altland farm, nobody was around, but Rom was browsing at the edge of the woods and I could hear voices. I left Diddle in the meadow and found Chav and Baval and Chavali down by the river with some liquid soap, a slime green kind I recognized. It was meant for hands, but they were using it to wash their clothes.

I said hi and watched awhile. The little kids were laughing and splashing water. Whenever they were around Chav they seemed to just assume that everything was okay, that he would take care of them. And I figured maybe they were right. But doing it had to weigh him down, like a colt carrying triple.

He wasn't talking. "You got the soap from a rest room at school, right?" I asked him.

He looked up. "Right." There was a sneer in his

51

voice, and his eyes dared me to make something of it.

I sat down on the ground, and he kept washing what was probably his total wardrobe: an extra pair of pants and two shirts. His clothes were crummy, but they matched. That is to say, they were all black.

"Why do you just wear black?" I asked him.

"I like black. It stands for death, and death is where the good people are."

Some of the kids at school wore weird styles and said things like that to shock the adults. But Chav wasn't saying it to shock me. He meant it.

I said, "My mother is dead too."

Where did that come from all of a sudden? I hadn't meant to say that. I hadn't even realized I believed part of his story, that his mother had died, like mine.

He stopped sloshing clothes and looked at me. Baval and Chavali got quiet and looked at me too.

I said, "My mother and father and brother all died."

They didn't say anything, just pulled their clothes out of the water and hung them on bushes and headed back up to their castle. But somehow their silence told me it was okay for me to be visiting them again.

"We've got lunch," Baval announced when we got to the silo, all excited, as if having lunch was something special. He pulled me through the crawlway and showed me a pile of cold, soggy, squashed, paper-wrapped McDonald's burgers.

"Chav got them," Chavali said, squatting there and holding one of the packets in both hands as if it were precious.

"He bought them?" I was thinking he ought to get his money back.

"Rom and I got them out of the Dumpster," he answered me from outside. "At two in the morning." Again his voice challenged me to try to make him feel ashamed.

"Well, will they keep till supper?" I said just as sharply. "I brought lunch."

I unloaded my pockets, and Chav let the little kids grab bologna sandwiches to eat, and then I jerked my head at him. I wanted to talk to him alone for a minute. We walked up the meadow toward where the horses were grazing.

"Mr. Fischel knows you're here," I said. "Except he thinks you're a whole tribe of Gypsies. He says you thieve."

"I do," Chav said, looking straight at me, his head high and cocky, his eyes hard. Tough, but— was he daring me to believe in him? "Isn't that what Gypsies do? Lie and thieve?"

"You—you steal things?"

"Clothes out of the Goodwill bin. Blankets out of barns. McDonald's burgers." There was mockery in his voice.

I found I was on his side. I mean, what else was

53

he supposed to do? If he tried to get a job and work, people would be like Mrs. Higby, wanting to know his whole name, where he lived, his social security number. And these were things he could not let anybody find out. For his own reasons. Probably good reasons.

I told him, "Mr. Fischel wants Mr. Altland to run you off."

"What else is new?" Chav said in the same scornful tone.

"Just telling you."

"Okay, I hear you. Who's this Fischel guy?"

I explained, and when I was done explaining we both stood there awhile patting the horses. Rom was really beautiful in his rawboned stallion way. Big Roman head, strong legs, short back, slim ribby barrel tucked at the flank. Wild shaggy mane like a mustang's. Like Chav's. Marks on his shoulders. I asked, "How did he get the scars?"

"Fighting." The hardness in Chav's voice, I decided, was aimed at the world in general. There was no need for me to snarl back at him. "Rom is like me, he has had to learn how to fight. Fight or be screwed."

"Fighting other horses?"

"Yes." He rolled his eyes—okay, it was a dumb question. "In my case, fighting people who try to hurt me or Chavali or Baval. Or Rom. No one touches Rom."

Almost no one. I stood there rubbing the black horse's neck, and he liked it. "What breed is he?"

"Gypsy."

It wasn't any breed I'd ever heard of. Was Chav a liar, the way he claimed to be?

"That's what *Rom* means," Chav added. "That he's a Gypsy horse."

No, Chav was not a liar. He was just—a poet. He had his own ways of saying truth.

"Where did you get him?"

A liar would have made up a story. But Chav sighed, and his voice was quiet, almost friendly, as he said, "I can't tell you."

I patted Rom and watched Chav awhile, and then I asked him, "Are you coming to school tomorrow?"

"Yes."

Journal   *Language Arts*
Oct. 22   *Mrs. Higby*
Chav

Yesterday after school Matt Kain and Fishy Fischel and some of their friends cornered me out back of the gym and tried to mess me up. They have heard I am a Gypsy, and that gives them an excuse to do what they want to me—as if they need a reason; I am different, that is reason enough. They called me "crooked Gyp" and all the usual names and beat me a few minutes before they got frightened and ran. I hurt them some, and I stayed on my feet.

They were not able to put me on the ground. But now I ache, every bone that has ever been broken aches, and it is hard to act as if nothing bothers me.

Gypsy, hell. I call myself a son of the Rom, but the stupid thing is, if I ever found my mother's people, they would call me "stinking gadjo" and drive me away. So I don't try to find them, not really. And I don't think too much. When I think too much about the way my life really is, it drives me crazy.

I don't think the gadjo jocks know about Baval and Chavali yet. They can do what they want to me, but they had better not bother Baval and Chavali, or I will kill them.

I must make up my mind to leave this place soon, or the weather will make it up for me. I think I am staying because I like the color of the leaves. It reminds me of hell.

✣   ✣   ✣

Journal   *Language Arts*
October 22   *Mrs. Higby*
Gray Calderone
Today in science lab our team was supposed to be separating a mixture of sand and iron filings and salt and stuff, and

Fishy Fischel, who is kind of a Peck Fischel clone, was being tough stuff and goofing around, so I said, "Stop it," because if he messed up the experiment, we'd all get a bad grade, and he stopped it, but he called me an obnoxious bitch. Just for saying what I thought. If I were a guy, I don't think he would have done that. Or maybe if I were a guy, I wouldn't have let him.

Actually I can't imagine being a guy, with my ego hanging out all the time. I wish Adam were here. He would explain things to me, like why guys put girls down and call them sluts and airheads. I guess not all guys have to be like that. Adam wasn't. He really cared about people, all people, even his pest of a little sister. I used to go along with him to play tag football or whatever, and the other boys would try to make me go away, but Adam would say, "Let her alone, she's as good as you are." Then they would laugh as if he were insulting them, but I don't think he meant it that way.

Why do girls and boys have to be so different? Boys get a stadium, girls get a hockey field. Boys get sports cars, girls get horses. Not that that's bad. But why is it only girls love horses? The only guy I've ever met who understands about horses besides Topher is Chav.

I can't figure Chav out. He's not like the other jerkhead boys, but he's not like Adam either, except that he cares about Baval and Chavali. That, and one of these days he's going to leave and I'll never see him again and I'll spend my life missing him the way I miss Adam.

❈   ❈   ❈

When I got home from school and there was a cop car in the driveway, I should have known right away that things were about to go wrong. But I wasn't worried at first.

"Hi, Grandpa," I said as I walked in the kitchen door and dumped my book bag on the table.

"Hey hey, Gray."

He sounded real glad to see me. But I saw he had his tie on, and that tipped me off, because usually when he came in the house he unclipped it and laid it somewhere. Not like he was ever off duty—a cop is a cop all the time—but sometimes he was more Grandpa and less cop, and this didn't look like one of those times.

"Give me a hug." Grandpa grabbed me. I hugged him back, but I ducked away when he tried to rub me with his whiskers, and I said, "What's going on?"

"Can't pull the wool over your eyes." He tried to joke around. "No flies on you." I kept looking at him, and he said, "I'm just killing a little time before I go back out to the old Altland place.

Nobody home the first time. Just some smelly blankets. Somebody's been squatting there. And horse piles." He asked me, "You know if anybody's been keeping a horse out there?"

He wasn't killing time, really. He was questioning me. I tried not to panic or lie. I just said, "Why would I?"

"I thought you knew every horse in three counties. You and Minda ever ride out there?"

"No." It wasn't a lie, because Minda never went with me. Before he could ask me another question I tried to find out what was going on. "Did Mr. Fischel call you or something? He says there's Gypsies camping there."

"I don't always believe everything Peck Fischel says, but he's got a right to be upset." Grandpa sat down at the table. "Somebody vandalized his family burial plot last night."

"Knocked down the headstones," my aunt said. I hadn't noticed how quiet she was, but now I understood why. There were tears in her voice. "Broke some of them. That's a terrible thing to do."

"Nobody's going to do that to Dan's grave," Grandpa told her, and he reached across to hold her hand. "Or Carrie's, or Cassie's."

At the time I was just worrying about Chav, I didn't really understand how the adults felt. Later on, when I saw the white marble angels lying in the dirt with their heads broken off, I began to understand.

I said to Grandpa, "Mr. Fischel thinks the Gypsies did it? Why would they?"

Grandpa squeezed my aunt's hand, then let go and got up again, like he was getting ready to leave. "From what I hear it's just three kids out at the Altland place, not a tribe of Gypsies."

I got scared and furious at the same time. "So why would they do it?" I yelled. "Why does everybody always have to blame everything on kids and Gypsies?"

First he looked mad that I yelled at him, but then he started to chuckle. "Kids and Gypsies," he laughed.

"Well, why do they?" Then I made myself calm down. "Do you think they did it?"

He shrugged. "I won't know until I find out. But even if they didn't, they're probably runaways. And they're trespassing on the Altland place."

Trying to make it sound like I was just kind of joking around, I said, "So what do you do with trespassing runaways? Take them to jail?"

"Take them to Children and Youth Services, probably."

I knew right then I had to do something. I wasn't stupid—I knew Chav had stolen Rom. They would find out and put him in a juvenile delinquent home, which meant they would take Baval and Chavali away from him, and that was the worst thing that could happen to him. Without his brother and sister—without his brother and sister

I didn't know what Chav would do. I just knew I couldn't let it happen.

Trying to make my voice stay calm and light, I said to Grandpa, "You going out there now?"

"Yep."

"Give me a ride as far as the stable?"

*   *   *

On the way I said to Grandpa, real casual, "You might want to talk to Topher."

"Who?"

"Topher Worthwine. The guy who runs the stable. He might know something."

"Why would he?"

I shrugged. "I just think he might. He lives right across the hill from the cemetery. He might have seen something."

Trying not to show it, I was almost holding my breath. Everything depended on this. If Grandpa went straight to the Altland place I'd never make it in time.

"Huh," was all Grandpa said. And I knew I didn't dare push it anymore. If I overdid it, he'd get suspicious. I stayed quiet, but I was so scared my hands were cold.

When we got to the stable Grandpa got out of his car and went looking for Topher.

It had worked! I ran out to fetch Diddle and hustled her to the barn and slung the saddle on her without even brushing. Now my hands weren't cold, but they were shaking. Getting Grandpa out of the car gave me a couple of extra minutes, but was that going to be enough?

By the time Grandpa left I was leading Diddle out of the stable. Grandpa had to drive down the road and turn onto another road and then a long rutted axle-breaker of a lane to reach the old Altland place. With a little luck I might just get there before him.

Topher gave me a strange look when he saw me getting on Diddle in such a rush. He asked, "Does all this hurry happen to have anything to do with the Gypsy kids?"

"Why would it?" This was turning out to be a good comeback for almost everything. And before he could answer I got out of there at a trot.

I put Diddle into a canter up the hill past the cemetery—and even at a canter I saw all the markers knocked down, and ugly words spray painted on some of them, and seeing it hit me like a slap. I felt my stomach start to ache. If anybody ever did that to Adam's grave, I'd—I'd—I didn't know what I'd do. Cry, probably. As if I hadn't cried enough. It probably was kids who did it too. Kids didn't believe in death, they didn't understand unless they loved somebody who had died.

But Chav was not like that. He believed in death—he wore black for death. He had loved his mother who had died. He couldn't have done this.

After we got past the cemetery and down the

hill Diddle really stretched out her fat furry little body and galloped. She must have felt some of what I was feeling, because she had never run like that before.

I slowed her down to a trot on the gravel of the railroad tracks, then ran her again when we reached the meadow. Rom was grazing not far away, and I didn't see any sign of Grandpa yet. I was in time.

"Chav," I yelled. I couldn't see him anywhere. But then there was movement in the dark entry to the silo. I saw Chav look out at me a moment, then turn away.

"Chav, come on!" I cantered over and pulled Diddle to a cowboy halt. "The cops are coming. You've got to get out of here."

He didn't answer or look at me again. All I could see was the back of his shoulder, bent over.

"Chav, the cops are coming!" Was he deaf or what? I didn't want to get down from Diddle, because then I'd just waste time getting back on her again, but it looked like I'd have to. I jumped down, let her reins drag to ground-tie her, and ducked into the silo.

"Chav, are you crazy? Get a move on!"

He didn't seem to hear me. He said something, but it wasn't like he was saying it to me. "She's sick," he said hoarsely.

It was hard to see much in there—too dark. All I could tell was that Baval was crouched against the back wall and Chav was holding Chavali in his arms.

"She's sick," he said again. "She's really sick." He sounded like he might break in half any minute. "I should have gotten her out of here. It's my fault."

CHAPTER

— 6 —

"Get her out where I can see her," I said.

I said it twice, and he moved like a sleepwalker, but he did it. He had Chavali wrapped in a blanket, so all I could see was her face. She kept her eyes closed, and she was flushed, feverish, and there were little red spots all over her cheeks.

"Chicken pox." I wasn't just guessing, I was sure, because I remembered from when I had it. You could tell by the blister in the middle of each red spot. It wasn't anything serious—chicken pox wouldn't kill anybody. When I had it, my mother called family practice and they didn't even want to see me. They made sure there were blisters in the middle of my spots, and then they just told her to keep me in bed and not let me scratch. Chavali was going to be okay. I had to take a couple of deep breaths, though, before I could stop being scared.

65

"Give her here," I said as I gathered Diddle's reins and swung up into the saddle.

Chav just stood there looking at me. I reached down and lifted Chavali out of his arms—wow, she was hot. The first thing to do would be to get her fever down. She peeked at me once, then played possum again because she didn't feel good. I cradled her in front of me with one hand and picked up the reins with the other. "Get on Rom," I told Chav.

He didn't move. Baval was dragging blankets and clothes out of the silo, trying to bundle them up. "Leave that stuff," I snapped, and I started Diddle toward the tracks. "Both of you get on Rom and come *on!*"

I heard the car coming in low gear down the lane.

Chav must have heard it too, and he finally got himself in gear. He ran and vaulted onto Rom, and gave Baval a hand to help him up behind him—he didn't even bother with the halter and the rope reins. He guided Rom with his knees and headed for the closest hiding place, the woods. I kicked Diddle into a reckless canter and followed, hanging on to the horse with my legs and Chavali with my arms. For a minute it felt like I was going to either fall off or drop Chavali, and I was scared silly again.

Then I was ducking branches. Hidden in the trees, I pulled Diddle to a walk, got myself collected, and looked back over my shoulder. Grandpa's cruiser was just nosing out from behind the farmhouse.

"Sheesh," I breathed. Another minute and he would have seen us.

Up ahead, Chav slipped off his belt and put it around Rom's neck and pulled on it to slow down the black horse so that it walked next to Diddle. He looked over at Chavali with a hard face. "Is she breathing?" he asked, and I realized his face got hard like that when he was afraid. His voice was tight as a drum.

"Of course she's breathing."

"Where are we going?"

"My place. We'll put her to bed. Get her some medicine."

"It's my fault she's sick." Now his voice sounded dead. "If I'd gone south when I should have, she would have stayed warm, it wouldn't have happened."

"Yes, it would've," I told him. "Everybody gets chicken pox. She'll be okay."

We came out of the woods, rode down the tracks, and then cut across the fields toward the stable. Not too fast—my heart was thumping with hurry, even Diddle wanted to hurry, but I held her in. We had to be careful with me carrying Chavali.

I was so intent on Chavali that we got within sight of the Fischel family cemetery before I remembered how this had all started. "Oh my

God. Chav, listen, they think you pushed over the stones in Mr. Fischel's graveyard."

"Huh?" He didn't know what I was talking about.

We were close enough so I could point to the broken angels. Then he understood, and his face flushed, and he said angrily, "They think I did that?"

"Mr. Fischel wants to blame it on the Gypsies."

"They're crazy. I wouldn't do that to dead people." He had his voice under control, but I could practically hear the black horse of anger thundering in his chest, and the black horse he was riding must have heard it too. Rom started to swerve and plunge.

"Go easy," Baval said softly, hanging onto his brother's back. "Everything will be all right."

Chav didn't answer. Rom settled down some, but he was still prancing when we got to the stable. Topher watched us ride in—he was standing there holding the hose, filling water troughs. His sandy-brown eyes widened when he saw Chav guiding the stallion with nothing but a belt looped around its neck. "Whooooa, boy," he said softly, leaving what he was doing and coming over, putting out a hand to get hold of Rom.

"Never mind them! Chav can handle it," I called. "Come help me with Chavali." I had definitely taken charge, which I guess some people would call being an obnoxious bitch. But Topher did what I said. When I handed the sick little girl down to him his mouth opened as wide as his eyes.

"What the hell—"

"I have to call my aunt," I said.

"This kid's sick."

"I know. Topher, can you keep Rom here for a few days? The black horse."

He blinked about five times, but then he nodded. Later he told me it was the way Chav rode the horse that made him do it. He had a prejudice: he just knew a boy who rode like that couldn't be all bad, no matter what Peck Fischel said. "Stick him in a stall," he called to Chav. "I'll drive you," he told me. "It'll be faster."

Chav came and took Chavali from Topher instead of sticking Rom in a stall. Rom started to wander off. Chavali started to cry. The water trough started to overflow. Things were confusing for a few minutes. When they sorted out, the water was turned off, the horses were in stalls, and we were all in Topher's Blazer, with Chav in the back holding Chavali on his lap.

"Emergency room, I assume," said Topher as he gunned it up the driveway.

"No!" Chav sounded panicky at the idea. People would ask him questions there.

"Just take us home," I told Topher. "Lee will know what to do. It's just chicken pox."

"You sure?"

"Positive." I explained to him why I felt so sure, and he believed me. That was another reason I liked Topher. He pretty much trusted me, the way Liana did.

"But—what's your aunt going to think of all this?" He meant Chav and Baval and Chavali, I guess, all of whom—well, in the closed car a person could really tell they needed a bath and a change of clothes.

"She'll be cool. You'll see." I wasn't as sure as I hoped I sounded, but it turned out I was right. When we went into the house, Liana was in the kitchen baking homemade bread, and she looked up and saw Chav standing there with that hard, haunted look in his eyes and his little sister in his arms, and that was all it took.

I said, "Lee, this is Chav and Baval and Chavali—"

"Chicken pox," she said.

"—and they don't have anyplace else to go."

She was already wiping the bread dough off her hands. "Go turn up the heat in the spare bedrooms. Chav, follow Gray, take your sister on back the hall; we'll get her in a bed." Her voice was very gentle when she spoke to him. "Do we still have Children's Tylenol?" she asked me, or maybe herself, since I was on my way out of the room. "No, I bet we don't. Or oatmeal bath, or Caladryl ointment . . ."

"You need some things?" Topher asked her. "I'll go get them."

"Would you?" She sounded surprised and glad to see him there. "I'll give you the money."

"No, you won't. And any other kind of help you need, you call me. I feel responsible, bringing this passel of God-knows-what in here."

I missed the rest, getting a thermometer for Chavali. Chav wouldn't put her down. Instead of tucking her into the ruffled bed in the peach-colored bedroom that used to belong to Cassie, he sat on it and held her. Baval said, "Chill out, bro," and sat beside him.

"One-oh-three," Liana read the thermometer a few minutes later. "That's not so bad, but let's get her in a tub of tepid water to bring that down." She peeled back some of the blankets and said straight to Chavali, "Is that okay, honey? Will you come with me and get a bath to make you feel better?"

It was like a little miracle. Chavali, the shy one, smiled and held out her arms.

*   *   *

A couple of hours later, after chicken soup and a dose of Tylenol and an oatmeal bath and some Caladryl ointment on her spots, Chavali really was feeling better. In fact, she was feeling good enough to make Chav do something he didn't want to do.

"Story!"

"Not right now."

"Yes, right now!"

"C'mon, sis. Give me a break."

They were in the peach bedroom, with Chavali snug in the bed now, and Liana and I were out in the kitchen putting things away after a late supper. Their voices floated down the hallway to us.

"I can't," Chav was saying. His voice sounded very tired. "Baval, you tell it to her."

"You tell her. You're the one who remembers."

I looked at Liana, and my eyes signaled, That's strange. Baval was old enough to remember most of what Chav did.

She nodded and stopped banging bread pans. We both eavesdropped.

"Listen," Chav said, "how about a new story?"

This must have been okay with Chavali. There was a silence and a rustling of the quilt while Chav stalled for time by getting himself settled on her bed. "This is a story about the night," he said.

"Why?"

"Because in a minute I am going to turn off the light and you are going to go to sleep. And it will be night in here. Now, listen. In a stable there is a black horse in the black night."

"Rom? Our black horse Rom?"

"Yes, Rom. The black horse is in the stall in the strange stable all by himself, and he's a little scared. So he listens hard, like this."

washing and drying their clothes while they're in bed. You can talk to them in the morning."

"Maybe you're not understanding me," Grandpa said between clenched teeth. "Read my lips. Get them out here *now*."

"This is my house," Liana said in a hard tone I had never heard from her before. "Do you have a warrant?"

I dared a look at them, and I could see Grandpa begin to realize Liana was really going to stand up to him. And she was his daughter, so he didn't want to get into a big fight with her. But he was a guy with his ego hanging out. He couldn't back down now. "I can go get one," he threatened.

"Bull. What have these kids done?" Liana puffed out a breath between her lips and let go of the hardness in her voice. "Sit down and have a cup of coffee, Dad," she said very gently. "There's no way I'm going to let you near them when you're all fussed up like a stampeding buffalo. If you'd seen them, you'd understand."

I guess he didn't want to lock horns with her anymore. He actually did what she said—he sat down. But now he was scowling at me.

"My own granddaughter," he said. "I sat out there in the cold for hours waiting for those squatters to come back before I started to get it. And then I couldn't believe it. My own granddaughter, making a fool of me."

"Sorry, Grandpa," I mumbled, feeling really bad that I hadn't thought before about what he'd do or how he'd feel. I guess I just kind of figured Grandpa would survive, but Chav might not. "I couldn't let you take them to the juvenile home."

"Why the hell not?"

"Because Chav—you might as well kill him."

"Chav's the oldest one," Liana said, giving Grandpa his cup of coffee. "He takes care of the little ones like a mama hen, but he really needs somebody to take care of him."

"Something terrible happened to him," I told Grandpa. "He has all kinds of scars, like he was in some kind of horrible accident, or maybe a fire."

Liana gave me a strange look. "No," she said. "No, I can see why you might think that, but that doesn't account for all of it."

"All of what?" Grandpa looked at the cup of coffee in his hands and set it down. "No damn coffee," he grumped.

"It's decaf."

"I don't care. I don't need it. All of what?"

"The look in his eyes," Liana said. "I think he's had awful things done to him. I think at the very least he was abused. Beaten."

At first when she said that I couldn't think or breathe. Then a minute later it all made sense, everything about Chav, but understanding it felt like somebody was beating on me. I hurt all over and had to curl up. Oh my God. Who could do such a thing to a beautiful child named Chav?

Grandpa was staring up at Liana, looking shocked. "You don't want that kind of kid in your house," he told her, though not like he was angry at her anymore—instead he sounded scared. "You could wake up with a knife at your throat."

"Dad, that's ridiculous."

"No, it's not. There's a pattern with these battered kids, and that pattern is that they turn out just like the people who did it to them. They don't care what happens to them, and they've got so much rage and pain—where do you think mass murderers come from, and serial killers? Hitler was abused as a child. Show me a violent criminal and I'll show you somebody who was abused as a child."

"But the pattern can be broken," Liana said. "Not every abused child turns into a criminal."

"The point is, you're taking a terrible chance." He was serious, pleading with her.

"I'll risk it."

"Liana, you're my daughter! I don't want to risk it. Let me get him out of here."

"Isn't he innocent until proved guilty?"

"All I'm saying is, let the professionals take care of him."

"No. He came to me."

"Liana, be reasonable!"

She stood up and said, "If I were reasonable, I

would have given up a long time ago. I need to live my life, Dad. Now, if you're not going to drink your coffee, go on home and go to bed. You can come back in the morning."

There was some more yelling. That is, he yelled. She never raised her voice at him. But in the end he did what she said.

CHAPTER

— 7 —

In the dead of night Chav lay tensely awake,
staring into the darkness.

Certain the gadjos were asleep at last, he swung
his bare feet out of the double bed he was sharing
with Baval. His brother immediately took over the
whole bed, still sleeping soundly. Baval could sleep
through anything, but some nights Chav hardly
slept at all, and this was one of them. Restless, he
padded into the hallway.

The feeling in his chest tonight was not so
much pressure as pain because Chavali was sick
and it was all his fault. Now here he was back in a
house again—his mind knew it was better for
Chavali to be in a warm bed under a roof, but the
rest of him was in a panic, screaming to run, run.
Once he had lived in a house like this, even bigger
than this, and he remembered being thrown
against its walls, and he remembered how blood

had looked, splattered on its carpeted floors. His blood. His mother's blood.

Houses were places where terrible things could happen. They had locks on the doors. They had walls to hide from the world what went on inside.

Chav walked softly toward Chavali's room. Being on the move helped him feel a little better—it would be harder for punishment to find him if he was moving. In the peach-colored bedroom he stood awhile listening to his sister's peaceful breathing. By the dim glow of her night-light he could not see the rash all over her, even on her eyelids. That helped some. But looking at her small face was like looking at angel goodness, at perfection. He did not deserve to be her brother. He had to leave her room.

Back down the hallway he barefooted, glancing into doorways as he passed them—Baval's room again, the bathroom, and Gray's room, where a hundred model horses stood alertly watching her sleep. All those plastic horses, but no real ones. Rom was far from here, out in the stable. Chav wished he were there with the horse, sleeping in the hay. He wouldn't have minded the cold—shivering with cold was better than shaking with fear inside a gadjo house. He hoped the black horse was okay. Did not feel at all sure, no matter what sort of story he told Chavali. Did not trust Topher or Gray. Did not like having to trust anyone.

She was a strange gadjo, that Gray. Tall—she

80

looked like a clown riding that ponyish Diddle. Big and bossy—but there was poetry in her too. And she seemed to care about—things. Maybe. Maybe not. It had been a long time since Chav had felt that sort of caring coming his way from anyone, and it frightened him. Because he had been born a bad person, the one person in the world who cared about him had been taken away, and he did not want to feel such grief and pain ever again.

He walked past the sweet-faced gadjo woman's room. Her hair was light-colored and permed, her eyes blue, her skin pale; nothing about her was at all like his small brown mother, yet she reminded Chav so much of his mother that it hurt.

This feeling also scared him. It sent him hurrying into the shadowy living room, with its tall windows, and beyond, to the glassy glittering dining room, the dark kitchen. He could not escape outside, as he would have liked—Chavali might wake up and need him. But his discomfort sent him prowling, on the hunt for something, he did not know what.

Without turning on any lights he found the rack full of kitchen knives. He found no guns, no clubs or whips or chains, but he found the cupboard full of drain cleaners and poisons. Still in the dark, he found the basement stairs and went down there and found the circuit breaker box and the alcove where the gardening supplies were kept, weed killers, chemicals. Back in the living room he discovered the coat closet. It was very dark in there. He burrowed to the back wall, behind the thick coats, and he closed the door. Good, no one would hear him, even if he screamed. No gadjo would care if he rotted in here. In the midnight blackness he started softly to sing:

> *"Hey hey far away*
> *I can hear her call to me*
> *Shady lady in the sky*
> *Help me spread my wings and fly*
> *Most days I just want to die. . . ."*

Grandpa came back early in the morning, before school, and brought the clothes and stuff that were left at the Altland place. He was quiet and polite when he said hi to me and when he asked Chav his questions. Chav was quiet and polite when he didn't answer them—he didn't tell Grandpa a thing, not even his name. Baval was happy and polite and told Grandpa he was the son of a Gypsy princess and he was looking for his real father. Lee was cheerful and polite and she made all of us French toast and scrambled eggs. Grandpa kept his tie on and wouldn't eat any. Chav didn't eat any either, just helped Chavali with hers. He seemed wound too tight to talk or eat.

As soon as Grandpa left I called Minda and

caught her still at home. "Listen," I told her, "you and I have had a fight."

"We have?"

"Yep. A humongous fight. So you're not speaking to me in school today. Hang around other people."

She said plaintively, "Am I allowed to ask why?"

"Sure. Ask."

"Why?"

"Because I need you to find out who wrecked up Mr. Fischel's cemetery. People are blaming Chav."

Silence.

"Minda?"

She said, "I'm just trying to figure out what it is with you and Chav."

"Well, he's living at my house right now, for starters."

"He's *what*?"

"I'll tell you all about it later." Much later. "Will you do it?"

"Do what?"

"What I said! Find out who trashed the grave-yard."

"Why not?" She sounded as if she were getting into it now. It's not every day a person has a chance to be an investigator. "If I'm allowed to bad-mouth you," she added.

"Absolutely." It was the best way to get information. People would see Chav come to school with me. If they wanted him to get blamed, they might not say things in front of Minda if she was still my friend. But if she was against me, they might.

As soon as I hung up, Topher called and talked with Liana, wanting to know if she needed anything or if there was any way he could help. "Topher says tell you Rom is fine, Chav," she called after us as we headed out the door. He nodded, but he didn't really seem to hear her.

∗ ∗ ∗

It took me a few days to realize how much better Liana was. She made homemade soup. She brought down boxes of picture books from the attic and read to Chavali for hours. She got a neighbor to baby-sit Chavali and went shopping and brought home armloads of new clothes for Baval and Chavali and even Chav, bright red and yellow and blue ones for them, black ones for him. Topher came over and she fed him lunch. She helped Chav and Baval with their homework and let them help her with the dishes. In the mornings she got up and wanted to see how everybody was doing. She picked up Chav and Baval and me at school in the afternoons when the weather was bad, and she wanted to know how it went. She got us to help her fix huge suppers, and she hummed while she was cooking them.

Something was making Lee feel a lot better.

The reason it took me a few days to notice all this was that I was worried about Chav. He wasn't

84

saying much to anybody. Not that he was being rude or mean. He thanked Liana for the clothes, and he wore them. But all the time he went around with a strange stretched-tight look like something was threatening to tear him apart.

I tried to get him to talk to me. "I guess you've missed a lot of school," I said while we were doing algebra at the kitchen table. He was flunking, but who cared? I mean, does anybody anywhere except teachers actually use algebra in their life?

Chav didn't say anything.

"Good thing you're not still living in a silo," I tried again. It was pouring down rain outside, like it had been for the past three days, raining so hard we hadn't gone out to the stable at all.

No answer.

"You're older than me, right?"

This time he answered, sort of. He nodded.

"How old? About fifteen?"

Nod.

"What do you want to do once you're out of school?"

He gave me a what-the-hell-is-she-talking-about look, like it was not something he had ever thought about. Like the whole idea of his having a life was totally weird.

Liana was in the bathroom with Chavali, and Baval was in the living room watching TV, so nobody should have been listening in. All of a sudden I decided to go for broke.

"Chav. Is it true what Liana thinks, that some-body used to beat you?"

Baval came charging in. "It is not!" he yelled before Chav could answer.

Chav's face had gone hard. I had seen that look on him often before, but now I understood what it meant, and I thought, He must have spent a lot of his life being scared.

Baval kept yelling. "He got those scars to save us from a big goon carny," he hollered at me. "When we were in the circus. This big no-neck got drunk and wanted to hurt us, but Carl—I mean Chav—he jumped in the way and fought him. The guy was a foot and a half taller and he weighed about three hundred pounds, but every time he knocked Chav down Chav got up again and kept fighting him. He fought him and fought him and hit him and hit him and hit him until finally he wore him out and got him backed into a corner and hit him once real hard in the jaw and knocked him out."

Chav wouldn't look at me, and I could tell he wanted to just sink through the floor and disap-pear. He was a good fighter, but he wasn't Superman going *kapow*—he had never done any of this, it was another of his wild stories, and he knew I knew it. It was the first time I had ever seen him embarrassed. He was blushing like fire, red under his brown skin until his whole face turned the color of a brick. "Um, bro, listen," he said, his voice low and struggling, "that's not really the way it was."

Baval looked like he had been slapped. "Yes, it is!" he screamed. "You were bloody all over. I wrapped you up. I took care of you afterward."

"No, it's not."

"It is so!"

"Do you know what we did in the circus?"

"Sure! You were a horseback acrobat. Chavali rode a giraffe. I was a knife thrower."

"How come you didn't just throw a knife into the big goon and help me out?" Chav asked him.

Baval's face went tight as he tried to think, and now I got to see what he looked like when he was scared. His skin went gray. "Maybe I forgot my knives?" His voice squeaked, and he was shaking. "Maybe I didn't have my knives with me, was that it? C'mon, Chav, tell me! You remember."

Chav gave in. "Okay, that must have been it," he said softly. "Okay, all right, calm down."

"Don't *do* that! Don't tell it one way and then another!" Baval started to cry. Chav gathered his little brother into a hug and held him against his shoulder, and I guess it was bad enough that Baval was crying, but the look on Chav's face—he was a person caught in a trap and he couldn't see a way out. I couldn't take it. I had to get up and go see how Liana and Chavali were doing.

*   *   *

The day the rain finally cleared up, Chav and I walked home from school and there was Topher having coffee with Lee.

"You want to come ride?" he asked me. "I'll drive you."

"Yeah! Thanks!" That was really nice of him. He knew I would be going crazy without my horse fix, and he knew Liana wouldn't want to leave Chavali.

"I'll even bring you back. Just call me Topher the Chauffeur. How about you?" he asked Chav. "You want to come say hi to that snortin' black horse of yours?"

The answer should have been about the same as mine. But Chav surprised all of us. His face went flat and closed, and he shook his head.

"You sure?" Topher asked, managing to keep his voice halfway calm and quiet. "That's quite a horse you got there. You sure you don't want to come see him?"

Chav sat down at the kitchen table, hunched over.

"Chav," I just about yelled at him, "come on! I know you miss Rom."

He winced like I was hitting him. "Let him alone," Liana told me.

I didn't feel like I could just go ahead and eat a snack and get my boots on. I stood there. Nobody knew what to do or say.

Chav lifted his head and asked Liana, "Where's Baval?"

"He got sent home from school. His turn to be sick."

"Chicken pox?" I asked.

"Yeppers." She sounded cheerful about it. Now that Chavali was feeling a lot better, maybe she needed another sick kid to take care of. I am a nice enough person that I didn't shout hooray or anything, but I have to admit it was good news to me too. With Baval sick, Chav would not go away—yet.

I knew in my heart of hearts that someday soon Chav was going to go off like a firecracker. I kept hearing him walking around in the night, in the darkest midnight part of the night. That poem of his had told me that night was private and magical to him, so I never got up and asked him what he was doing. But that poem of his had told me other things about him as well.

I didn't want to think about them right then. "Chav," I coaxed, "Baval doesn't need you. Come on out to the stable and see Rom. You can go riding with me."

"No," he said. "Don't make me." He had that black-ice hard look on his face. Scared—but of what? Of Rom? Scared of the black horse?

CHAPTER

— 8 —

"Well," Topher complained, "if Chav doesn't want to ride him, I think I will."

I wasn't paying much attention because Minda was there and we were laughing and hugging. Nobody from school was watching at the stable, so we didn't have to pretend to hate each other.

"Did you find out anything?" I asked her when we got done hugging.

"Not yet. But at least I feel like there's something there to find out. You know how it is when people won't say anything, but they grin?"

"Like what people?"

"Matt Kain, mostly."

It figured. "Keep trying?"

"Sure. Now, you tell me. What is it with you and Chav?"

"Nothing, really."

"Oh, *sure*. Nothing?"

She had "boyfriend" on her mind, which wasn't true, but—I would never in a thousand years be able to explain to her what Chav meant to me, even if I knew for sure, which I didn't yet. "Minda, let's just ride, okay?"

I went out into the ankle-deep mud hole Topher called a paddock to catch Paradiddle, and Minda had to do the same thing to get Dude, and of course both horses had rolled. They even had mud caked in their ears. They looked so proud of themselves. We used the horse vacuum on them, but it still took us half an hour to clean them off. When we finally got them saddled up and let them out, there was Topher, cowboy hat and all, on Rom.

And Rom was dancing.

Not acting up. Dancing. Like a ballet horse. Minda and I stood gawking, and Topher sat arrow straight in the saddle with his legs down long around the horse, and I never saw his cowboy boots move or his hands move on the double reins, but Rom tucked his chin and arched his neck and strutted in place. Topher shifted balance ever so slightly and Rom waltzed six feet sideways, his front feet crossing over each other. Topher leaned back just a little and the horse pirouetted full circle on his hind feet.

"I just had a hunch." Topher loosened the rein and Rom stood still, and Topher patted him on his arched neck. "This horse is trained for upper-level dressage," he said. "He's like a fine-tuned machine. And he's a stud. He's been used for breeding. How the hell . . ."

He let the words trail away and didn't say it, but I could have said it for him: How the hell did a horse like that end up roaming the countryside with a Gypsy kid?

"C'mon, Minda," I muttered, and I turned away to go ride Diddle.

*   *   *

Grandpa came over that evening and accepted coffee and actually took off his tie and laid it beside his place mat. "Well, boy," he said sourly to Chav across the kitchen table, "you'll be glad to hear I haven't been able to find out a damn thing about you."

Chav just looked back at him, trying to hide what he was feeling, but relief flickered across his face anyway and his chest heaved. I saw.

So did Grandpa, probably. "How am I missing the boat?" he asked, not expecting anybody to answer. "You don't have a criminal record. I ran your prints. Got them off this." He handed a school notebook back to Chav. "You aren't a runaway. Or if you are, nobody's looking for you. Nobody's looking for anybody who matches you or those other two."

That should have felt awful, to be a kid on your own with nobody missing you, nobody who cared. But Chav sighed with relief again.

Grandpa was watching him. "Not that I think Chav is your real name," he added. "I'm not stupid."

"It's a Gypsy word," Chav told him quietly and courteously. "All it means is 'boy.' *Baval* means 'in the wind.' *Chavali* means 'little girl.' "

"So you plan to call yourself 'boy' all your life?"

Suddenly Chav was neither quiet nor courteous. "I'll never call myself by any stinking gadjo name," he said viciously. "Beat me bloody, why don't you?" He stood up so fast he knocked over his chair, and strode back down the hallway to where Liana and the little kids were.

Grandpa and I just sat. "I think it was a gadjo who did things to him," I said.

"What the hell is 'gadjo'?"

"Like you and me. Not Gypsy."

"He's hiding something," Grandpa said. "I can smell it."

I didn't say anything, but I knew exactly what Chav was hiding: Rom. Topher must not have told Grandpa about Rom, or Grandpa would have been checking for stolen horses.

Back down the hallway we could hear Chav start to sing for his brother and sister:

> *"Red horse, blue horse*
> *see you in the zoo horse*
> *black horse, white horse*
> *put up a hell of a fight horse*
> *pink horse, green horse . . ."*

The children were laughing. "Do you still think Chav is dangerous?" I asked Grandpa.

"Yes."

"And you're still mad at me." This time it wasn't a question. I could tell he was mad. He wouldn't say so, and he wouldn't even treat me much differently, but he would look straight at me—kind of through me, actually—and not smile.

"It's not so much that I'm mad," he said, which was a lie. "It's more that I just don't understand how you could do what you did."

"You mean because I went behind your back? Even if I'd told you all about Chav, you still would have wanted to put him in a juvenile home."

"Yes, because that's where he belongs! Not here. What I can't believe is what you're doing to Liana, bringing those kids here."

I goggled at him. "She likes having them here!" Surely he could see that.

"And how's she going to feel when they run away? Which is exactly what's going to happen."

"It will not," I said, but now I was the liar, because I knew he was right. I had heard Chav roaming in the night like a wild mustang penned in a corral. He wanted to run.

Well, I would just have to make him want to stay somehow, that was all. Baval was sick. Chav wouldn't go anywhere until he could take his brother and sister with him. I had a little time.

Journal   Language Arts
Oct. 31   Mrs. Higby
Chav

Today is Halloween. I hate it. How can people enjoy being scared? I don't need this—I am afraid all the time anyway. I look out of my own eyes, but everything seems strange. My thoughts are strange. My hands don't seem to belong to me. I am coming apart.

Matt Kain said to me, "Hey, ugly, don't go buying a mask. You can just wear your face and scare little kids." Little kids, hell. I scare me. I can't look in the mirror. I am terrified I might see who I really am.

Partly it is the goodness frightening me. Liana and Gray are so good to me I can't stand it. I don't deserve it. Can't they understand? Chavali was sick, and now Baval is. I am to blame, and I should be punished.

Sometimes when they have been gentle with me I forget, I have these stupid thoughts, like I might live. Or like there might be a heaven. Then I would have a farm like Topher's, and I would be the one who fed the animals, and they would all be black. Black horses, black sheep, black cats, glossy black goats, black rabbits, black birds flying around and singing.

Black brainless dogs barking and running everywhere. Black snakes in the sun, black mice in the barn. Just black animals with no white on them, and no other kind. And they would all want me to pat them.

Then I realize how dumb even thinking about it is, because there is no God for scum like me and I am going to die. Liana and Gray can take care of Chavali and Baval a lot better than I ever could. Soon they won't need me anymore. Then I can do it, what I've always planned I would. Get a gun. Go out with a bang. Take a lot of filthy gadjos with me. Matt Kain, for one.

I am frightened thinking about it, but I will do it. Dying doesn't scare me nearly as much as living this way.

*   *   *

"The self-presentation speech is required, Chav." That was Mrs. Higby, who had this idea that we should each talk about ourselves for a few minutes, I forget why.

"C'mon, Chav, you can do it!" That was Minda.

"C'mon, Chav." That was one of the other kids. Some of them were starting to talk to him a little.

"Chav, you've got to. Please." That was me. I'm not sure why I felt like he just had to do it, except that I wanted him to ace something so he'd feel better about himself. He was failing every subject, but I knew he could stand up and talk, because of his poem that first day. "If I help you?" I begged. "What if we do it like an interview? Mrs. Higby? Can we do that?"

"You *may* do that."

I detested her but didn't let it show. "Chav?" I stood up.

He sat slumped in his chair shutting us all out, but then he looked up at me. It was his black-ice look—I couldn't figure out what he was thinking. But then he stood up.

"All riiiight!" I led the way to the front of the room. Chav came with me.

Being a ham is one thing I know how to do. I held an imaginary mike to my mouth and went into ham mode, not to make fun of Chav but just to lighten things up. "Ladies and gentlemen, we have with us today an unusual kid named Chav. He is going to tell us a little bit about himself." I tried to think of a question he wouldn't mind answering. "Chav, is it true that you're a Gypsy?" I pointed the pretend mike at his mouth.

For a second I was afraid he wouldn't go along with it. He had his stretched-tight look on his face. But then he said, "Half true. My mother was a Gypsy."

"What's that make you, Gyp?" Matt Kain called.

Some people laughed. Chav did not look at anyone directly as he said, "You call Gypsies thieves. But Gypsies call themselves the tribes of Romany, the most ancient people in the world. They are

97

nomads—they have always lived off the land. Why should they change their way of life because everything is taken over by—"

Before he could say "gadjos," I took charge of the mike. "Does that mean you were raised, like, roaming all over the country?" It would explain a lot about him.

"No. My mother married a gadjo."

He said the word so bitterly I couldn't duck the next logical question. "Gadjo?"

"A white man. Not Gypsy." I took the "mike" away, but he stared straight ahead and kept talking. "So her tribe disowned her. It was a disgrace—her parents and her people turned their backs. She never saw them again. She lived with her rich gadjo in his big house, and when he started to beat her and break her bones there was nowhere for her to go."

The class went stone quiet. I felt like I was on a runaway horse, hanging on, supposedly in charge, but really things were out of control. Way out of control. Forget about the stupid interview game and the stupid pretend mike in my hand. I asked softly, "Are you talking about your father?"

"Don't call him that!" His eyes blazed into me. "I hate him."

I don't know how I got the nerve to say it. "He hurt you too."

He scowled at me and did not answer. Later I learned some of the things he was not saying. How badly his father had hurt him. How he had started to fight back, but it just made things worse. How he had wanted to kill his father but could not.

"So you ran away." It was safe to say this. If Grandpa could not trace him, nobody could.

"Yes."

"And you took Baval and Chavali with you."

"Somebody had to take care of them. Mom was—dead." His voice hung up for a moment when he said it, stuck like a raft on a rock, a hurt too hard for words. "I couldn't leave them with—him. So we all went. We've been on our own awhile now. It's rough." Everybody in the class was watching him with eyes wide open, and all of a sudden he glared back at them. "You guys complain about the food in the cafeteria—sometimes I've eaten out of garbage bags, I've eaten things people put out for their birdfeeders. You don't know how lucky you are, with warm rooms to sleep in and parents who—care about you. . . ."

His voice faltered and quit. He sagged back against the blackboard and leaned there and closed his eyes. I could see the lids trembling.

"Chav?" I took his hand and felt him quivering. "Chav, are you okay?"

"Chav." Minda left her seat and came and touched his shoulder. "Chav, it's over now."

"It's gonna be okay, Chav." Of all people, Matt Kain the Pain came up. A whole group of kids came up and clustered around. "Chav? It's okay now. You're gonna be okay."

"Take your seats, all of you," Mrs. Higby said,

but not too sharply for her. "Chav, you may sit down."

He didn't move at first, but then he opened his eyes, and they were burning dry, and he looked around at everybody in a kind of daze. He went back to his desk and sat like he wasn't hearing anything, like he was just barely hanging on, riding a runaway life.

"I shouldn't have made you do it," I told him when class was over.

"Nobody made me do anything."

That was kind of true. But I was worried, because I couldn't figure out why he had told us some of the truth about himself.

Was it a good sign? Was he getting ready to settle in, be friends, be one of us?

Or—was he getting ready for something else?

I couldn't explain it, but I felt trouble coming, I felt it like an ache in my bones, like the thickness in the air before a storm.

CHAPTER

— 9 —

When we got home there were huge dapple-red apples on the kitchen table.

"Chris brought them," Liana explained.

Huh? "Chris?"

"From the stable."

"Topher."

"He asked me to call him Chris." She was making an apple cobbler and humming. Chav went down the hallway to see Baval. I sat down and Chavali sat on my lap. Lee hummed some more, then said, "He says it's high time he got over Christina."

Liana sliced apples, but she wasn't humming now, she was thinking. And she wasn't saying what she was thinking. One thing I had noticed, being around Chav: sometimes what people don't say is as important as what they do. And what Lee wasn't saying was, maybe it was time she got over Uncle Dan.

Or maybe it was just me thinking that.

"Do you know why she left him?" Lee asked, and now she sounded mad. "Because he wouldn't give up his horses. Because she didn't like the way he loved them, she thought it took something away from her. Of all the stupid—how can you marry somebody and not want them to be who they are? Everybody's entitled to love what they love."

I snitched a slice of apple and offered it to Chavali. She grabbed it and grinned. Her chicken pox was almost gone, and it didn't look like she was going to have any scarring. Her face would stay as smooth and pretty as a tan flower.

"Like your uncle Dan and that boat of his," Lee said softly. "He was bone-deep happy when he was on it. He got a light in his eyes just talking about it. Even if I'd known it was going to kill him, I could never have tried to take it away. Loving it was part of what made him alive."

Her voice was quiet but steady. It was the first time I had heard her talk so calmly about what had happened, and it gave me an odd, lost feeling, like I was being left behind.

I blurted, "What do you love, Lee?"

"You."

That made me smile. She would never leave me behind, not really. It was just that she was moving on. "C'mon. I love horses. What do you love?"

She knew the answer, but it took her a while to

say it. She put the dough on the cobbler first. Then, "I think I love taking care of people," she said slowly. "Especially kids. I think maybe I need to go back to school to be a nurse or a therapist or something. I think you're what has kept me going these past two years, but I have to watch myself that I don't spoil you or smother you." Now she wanted to talk to me alone. "Chavali, 'Sesame Street' is on."

It worked. Chavali slid down from my lap and ran to the TV. Lee put her cobbler in the oven and sat down across from me. She came right to the point. "Gray, how would you feel if I adopted Baval and Chavali and Chav?"

It was funny, because in a way it was exactly what I wanted, but in another way it was a shock. Like, wasn't I kid enough for her?

What she said next made it worse. "I didn't realize how empty the house felt before you brought them here." Then she leaned toward me, happy, all glowy like a sunrise. "They fill it up. I don't know . . . maybe I want to keep them for all the wrong reasons, but I just—have you noticed I don't need to take pills anymore?"

I had noticed. "They fill up your heart," I said. She wasn't missing Carrie and Cassie and Uncle Dan so much anymore.

She touched my hand. "You're the one who brought them here. Thank you."

"It just happened," I grumped. "I didn't mean

to change everything." I hated the way it felt to want two things at once, which were, I wanted Chav to stay, but I wanted things to be the way they'd always been between Liana and me. "I'd kind of rather have you to myself."

She was watching me with the funniest smile on her face. "I kind of figured you might feel that way."

"And what about Grandpa? He'll think we're nuts. So will Grandma."

"Well, are they right?"

I had to smile back at her. "Sort of."

"It's true that I'll have less time for you if Chav and Baval and Chavali stay with us." Lee was trying to be fair, even though we both knew what she really wanted. "I might even have to get a job. And Gray, they've been so neglected, there are going to be a lot of medical bills and so on. There might not be enough money for a horse for you after all."

Ouch. That hurt.

Then I thought of something, and I was greedy and afraid both at once. Really, what I'd always wanted was a black stallion. And if Chav didn't want Rom anymore . . . "What about Chav's horse? Can we keep it?"

"I haven't figured that one out yet. Why won't Chav go to see it?"

"I don't know. Lee, I'm worried about Chav."

So was she. It turned out she had already made

an appointment for him to see a psychologist, starting in a few days. But I wondered how much good a person who didn't even know him could do, and how soon.

"Don't say anything to him yet about staying with us," she told me. "He's not ready."

"Don't worry. Neither am I."

Liana had stood up from the table to go on about her cooking, but now she looked at me, and then she crouched in front of me and looked at me some more. "Gray," she said, "take a couple of days to think it over, and then let me know how you feel, the truth, the whole truth, and nothing but the truth, okay?"

"Okay." I felt bad that I couldn't just say yes right away. "It's complicated."

"Yes, it is. Most important things are."

*　　*　　*

I didn't get a couple of days to think it over. I didn't even get a couple of hours. At suppertime Baval blew the whole thing wide open.

Apparently he had been doing some thinking on his own, lying around scratching his chicken pox. This was the first night he felt well enough to come out to the dining room and eat with the rest of us. Aside from the apple cobbler, Liana had cooked roast chicken with Pepperidge Farm stuffing, mashed potatoes and gravy, cranberry-orange relish, and baby carrots in some sort of butter

105

glaze. Baval got cranberry relish on his face, and we teased him that the color blended in with his chicken pox bumps. He laughed and laughed, and then for half a second he looked like he wanted to cry, and then straight to Lee he said, "I want to stay here when I get better. Please."

She never even blinked, because she couldn't let Baval down—I understood that right away. "I very much want you all to stay," she told him gently.

"I want to stay here," Baval said again, this time to his brother. "Carl, I mean Chav, I'm tired of looking for Father. I want us to just stay here with Liana."

Chav didn't say anything. To me it looked as if he couldn't. He had gone stiff, with eyes like a spooked colt's, wild and white and frightened.

"Let Father find us," Baval insisted.

"Or we can look for him when we're grown up," Chavali put in.

"Yeah. That's what we can do. I'm tired of eating garbage and being cold and not having a place to live." Baval's voice was high and a little shaky. This meant a lot to him. "I want to stay here where it's nice. Chavali, don't you want that too?"

She nodded very seriously, moving her pointed little chin once up, once down.

"Chav?" Baval pleaded. "Can we stay?"

Hanging on to the edge of the table, Chav opened his mouth but did not speak. It was like he was gasping for air, as if he felt like he was drowning.

"Let him alone, Baval," Lee said softly.

"But it's what he wants too! I know it is!" Baval's voice went so high it squeaked. He couldn't sit still—he headed around the table toward Chav, tripping in his new pajamas and bathrobe and slippers. "Isn't it, Chav? Isn't it what you always wanted? Somebody to give you good food and love you?"

"Baval, let him alone!"

That was me, for all the good it did. Chav had already heard more than he could bear. He couldn't take it. Trying to get away from the table, he knocked over his chair, staggering like he couldn't walk. He fell on the floor, curled up against the wall with his hands over his head as if people were hitting him. He was shaking all over.

"Chav!" I knelt down beside him and tried to hold him. He flinched away from me, hiding his face with his arms. Lee knelt down too and stroked his shoulders. Baval stood looking at all of us.

"But it's what he wants too!" Baval was trying not to cry. "What's the matter with him?"

"He'll be okay, Baval," Lee said. It sure didn't look like it—Chav was moaning. She tried to hug him, but he pulled away from her. She sighed and tried to explain to Baval, "You always had him to take care of you, but nobody was taking care of him. He's scared. He needs time."

"But—but Chav's never scared!"

"He just never showed you before," I said. "He couldn't."

Little Chavali came over and patted Chav's hair. He lay there a minute, but then he sat up and uncurled just enough to grab her and hug her and rock her as if she had been crying. She snuggled up against him, and the two of them stayed like that for a long time.

Liana knelt in front of them. "Chav," she requested, "please give it just a few more days. Until you get a chance to talk to the doctor." But he didn't answer her.

Dinner was only half eaten, but we cleared the table anyway. Nobody was hungry anymore.

I couldn't sleep that night.

*　*　*

Chav felt time ticking louder and louder inside his chest as if his whole body were a bomb wired to explode. A while after midnight he decided it was no use waiting any longer. Silent as a cat, he got up and walked to the room where they had put Baval when he got sick. He touched his younger brother on the shoulder. For once Baval sat up right away, wide-awake, as if he had been lying there awake.

"Things are bad when you can't sleep," Chav teased.

"Chav, please say we can stay." Baval's voice

quivered. He was almost twelve, but he acted like a little boy. Chav had noticed this before, but up until now it had been okay in a way. It was what Chav had wanted, to give Baval back some of his childhood. But now Baval had to grow up. Now everything was different, dangerous. Chav felt the darkness in his heart galloping harder and fiercer than ever before.

"You can stay." Chav's voice was gentle, because he meant it. "You and Chavali stay with Gray and Liana. They'll take good care of you." *Better than I ever did. I should have known I'd blow it. You were cold and hungry a lot of the time. You and Chavali got sick.*

"No, Chav!" The kid bolted up out of his covers. "You stay too."

"Don't try to find our father," Chav went on, hurrying to stay ahead of the black feeling that surged and pounded in his chest. "We don't have a Gypsy father. All those stories I told you were lies."

That's me. Typical Gypsy. A liar.

"No, they weren't! They weren't! They were good!"

"Shhhh. You're going to wake Liana." But what Chav needed to say was important enough that he had to keep going. He took his kid brother by the shoulders and pushed him down until he was sitting on the bed again. "Baval, you've got to listen to me just this once. Our real father used to beat the crap out of me, okay?"

109

"*No!* No, that's not true!" Baval's voice rose to a yell. He wasn't listening, just getting hysterical.

He can't bear it. Not what happened to Mom, not any of it. That's why he can't remember. He probably doesn't even remember his own real name anymore.

But someday he might.

Keeping his voice low and calm, Chav told him, "Listen, all I want you to understand is, don't go near him, okay?"

"No! No, you stay with me!"

"I can't," Chav said very softly. *Damn it, if you would face things, remember them, you would understand.*

Baval squirmed away from his hands, lunged off the other side of the bed, and started scrambling into his jeans.

"What the hell are you doing?"

"Coming—with you."

"Damn it, forget about me! I—I'm toilet paper, okay? Flush me down the john. Just stay here and be happy."

"You—try to go, I'll—follow you." Baval was crying.

There was a sound. Chav turned. Gray stood at the bedroom door.

She was wearing a big white T-shirt that used to belong to her dead father. She slept in those things, and to Chav they always made her look like an orphaned angel with its outgrown robe too short. A big, long-legged, clownish, plain-faced rescuing angel. The way he felt about Gray scared him to death.

She came in and hugged Baval to calm him down but looked straight at Chav. And she said what she was thinking straight out. That's the way she was.

"Don't go away," she said. "I know you like it here, I know you like Lee. And me, a little."

Her, a lot. Too much. He shook his head hard. "Liking I could handle," he said hoarsely. All his life he had liked people sometimes and left them behind. Damn his rich gadjo father, there had been homes in Florida, Virginia, New York. There had been private day schools, one after another. There had been horses, left behind. There had been friends and friends left behind. Liking was manageable.

But loving was not. If you let yourself love somebody, anybody, then you were in a trap, and terrible, terrible pain followed.

"What is it, Chav? Chav, tell me."

His face must have changed. She had stepped back. She looked frightened of him. It was bad, how sometimes things showed in his face.

No, it was good, because he was bad, clear through. That was why his father had punished him, because he was a bad person. They had to understand that.

Bad people lied. His poems and stories were all

just that, lies. For a while there he had wanted to tell the truth so that people would understand after he was gone, but why bother anymore? It would all be over soon. He would be a liar. That way they would hate him when they found out, they would not grieve, it would be easier on them.

"Nothing," he told Gray. "It's nothing."

Liana was peering in the doorway now too, and Chavali, holding Lee's hand. Chav didn't look at them, but he said to his brother, "Baval, go back to bed, go to sleep. I'm not going anywhere."

The kid looked up at him with his face red and blotched from chicken pox and crying. "You'll stay?"

"Yes," Chav lied. Well, it was true at least for a little while. He couldn't go anywhere that night, with everyone awake and watching him. He'd manage to wait a short while longer. Pick his time.

Baval cried at him, "You promise?"

"Yes." They would hate him for this, and that was good. Hate was good. It would make them forget him sooner. "Yes, I promise."

CHAPTER

—10—

The next morning was Saturday. I should have been sleeping in, but instead I was up at dawn, peeking into Chav's bedroom—yes, he was there, lying in his bed. Then another door creaked, and Liana looked out of her room at me.

"Gray," she whispered, beckoning to me.

I went in and we sat on her bed. "Are you okay?" she asked.

"Sure. Why wouldn't I be?"

"Well, I told you to think things over for a few days, but last night I promised Baval—"

"You had to," I told her.

"That's what I thought. But now Chav—"

I said, "You had to tell Baval yes. You know I'll be okay, but he needs help. So do Chavali and Chav."

"You want them to stay?"

"Yes!" There was no doubt in me anymore.

Every minute I didn't have Chav in my sight now I was afraid he had run away. If he left, I would never be able to forget him. I would spend my life wondering what had become of him. "Of course I do."

Lee smiled with relief, but her eyes got misty. "You are so much like your mother," she said. "So bighearted and strong."

Big-nosed would have been more like it. "Too bad I look like my dad."

"C'mon. My brother was a sweet man. He loved to read." Lee gave me a thoughtful look. "Did they ever tell you why they named you Grace?"

Of course they had, because I'd complained at them so often about how I hated my name. But I wanted to hear what Lee said. "I forget."

"Because it was your mother's mother's name— but also because of something a writer named Hemingway said. He defined courage as 'grace under pressure.' Not physical grace but a kind of—a kind of inner balance. So to them it was a name that meant courage. They knew you would be a brave person."

"Right," I said, being sarcastic.

"Gray, it's true. You are the gutsiest kid I know."

I shook my head. "Chav is," I said. "Taking Baval and Chavali with him when he ran away, and taking care of them for a year and a half, that's amazing, that's the gutsiest thing I ever heard of."

114

Most kids would have turned against their brothers and sisters, but Chav had given everything he had. And he was paying for it now.

On the way back to my room to get dressed, I checked on him. He was still lying there, but my heart pounded at the thought of losing him, my head hurt with thinking of how to help him get well. Grace under pressure, that was me.

*   *   *

Topher, I mean Chris, came over that morning, which was kind of unusual, because Saturday was his busy day. And when I opened the door and said hi he didn't smile, which was even more unusual. He carried his hat and a copy of *Horse Report* magazine with his finger stuck between the pages.

"Hi, Liana." He smiled at her, but the smile didn't quite reach his eyes. "I've got to talk to Chav."

"What's the matter, Chris?"

He didn't get a chance to tell her. Chav came into the living room like he had been standing in the hallway waiting for his cue. He held his face so still I could tell he had expected this visit all along, except that maybe he had figured it would come from Grandpa, not Topher.

Topher nodded at him, and he looked steadily back. They had barely ever talked, but somehow they seemed to understand each other.

"Is this about Rom?" Liana asked.

"It's okay," Chav said to her. What did that mean? It was okay if he went to jail? It was okay if he gave up and died?

"Been looking through my old mags," Topher said, mostly to Chav. "Took a while to find him." He opened the magazine to the page he was marking with his finger. I didn't want to look, because I knew what I'd see, but I had to look anyway. Sure enough. A big glossy picture of Rom, with "MISSING: Fuerza Epica of Spanish Dancer Ranch" printed underneath.

"He's a grand champion Spanish Barb," Topher said. "Worth about ninety thousand dollars."

That shook me. And I saw Liana turn pale. "Oh no," she whispered.

Everyone was staring at Chav. He looked through us. "They had him in a razor-wire pen," he said in that quiet, gritty way of his, "with this big pig-faced farm horse stud beating up on him. Too big for him to handle. Kicking him and driving him into the wire, cutting him open. He was bleeding all over. No way I was going to leave him in there."

Topher looked shocked and surprised. "There's no razor wire at the Spanish Dancer Ranch," he said. "I've been there."

"I'm telling you the truth." Chav's voice went so soft I knew he was scorching mad.

"I believe you. Give me some credit. Where did you find Rom? What state?"

Chav shook his head.

"For crying out loud, I'm not a cop. I'm not going to haul you away." Now Topher was a little mad, but he got past it. "Okay, what month, then?"

"Spring."

"You sure?"

"Yes. Warm weather."

"The horse has been missing since January." Topher gave Chav a quizzical look. "I think you stole him from whoever stole him in the first place."

Chav said nothing. "Is that better?" Liana asked Topher anxiously.

"Maybe not technically. But it makes me feel better." Topher gave Liana a one-armed hug at the same time he was giving Chav his wry look again. "Chav, we've got to get the horse back to Spanish Dancer Ranch."

Chav had that black-ice glare in his eyes, but he looked straight at Topher. "They will treat him right there? They will not beat him or put him in wire fence?"

"God, no." Topher let go of Liana and studied Chav. "You're quite a kid, you know? Anybody else would be asking what's going to happen to them, but you're worried about the horse."

"I don't care what happens to me."

Topher looked at Chav some more, then said, "The scary thing is, I almost believe that."

Chav said nothing.

"Well, I care, damn it," Topher said. "Will you let me handle it?"

Chav didn't say no.

Silence must have been answer enough. Topher headed toward the phone, then seemed to remember he was not at home. "Can I make a long-distance call?" he asked Liana. "I'll—"

"You will *not* pay for it," she snapped before he could offer. "For God's sake."

That made him grin as he dialed the number in the magazine ad. But he got serious as he waited for somebody to answer.

Somebody did. "Yes, this is about Fuerza Epica," Topher barked into the phone in a voice that didn't sound like his. "You want to know where he is, there's got to be no questions asked, or I'm hanging up right now. What? No, you're not putting me on hold. You heard what I said. Do I hang up?" He listened a moment. "Okay, do that. I'll call back."

He disconnected the phone with his finger and told us, "They're getting the boss."

Liana nodded. We were all standing there watching Topher, including Chav and Baval and Chavali. Nobody said a word. It was like we were afraid to say anything.

118

He called back in a few minutes, and this time apparently a different person answered the phone, and Topher said in his normal voice, a soft drawl, "Okay, no questions asked? Good. You want to write down some directions? No, it's okay, ma'am, you I trust." This was somebody he knew something about. He gave his name, phone number, and directions to his farm. "The horse hasn't been with me long," he said. "He's scarred up some, he's been mistreated, but not by anybody I know. Not recently. He seems fine now." A pause. "No, I can't tell you more. Sorry, ma'am. I'll expect you this evening, then."

He hung up and stood there looking at the phone.

Then he looked at Chav like he was trying to think of what to say. But all he came up with was, "Rom's going tonight."

Chav stood silent and rigid beside me, all dressed in black as if for a funeral, and I could practically hear his heart breaking. I snapped, "Topher, he *knows*. He *heard*."

Topher nodded, at me I guess, but he kept looking at Chav. Then he said, "I think you should come out to the stable with me. Say good-bye to him."

And Chav surprised all of us. He nodded and put on the new black winter jacket Liana had bought him and went with Topher.

I just stood there and watched them walk to the

car and didn't even ask to go along. Me, the all-time want-to-ride girl, staying home? But it seemed to me that this day for Chav was like the nights when he walked alone and sang to the darkness. It didn't include me.

Standing beside me, watching out the front window like I was, Baval said in a high, anxious voice, "He'll be back. He promised to stay."

"I want to stay too," said Chavali.

"That's right." I took her hand. "You're going to."

We watched Topher's beat-up Blazer drive off.

"He promised he'd stay," Baval said again the same way.

"That's right," I told him. I had heard Chav's promise too.

The sun was pouring in the window. Why did I feel so cold?

*   *   *

Topher's call came sometime after lunch. Just by the way Liana stood there after she answered the phone I knew something was wrong.

"I'll be right out, Chris." Those were nearly the only words she said. Then she hung up and grabbed for her jacket. "Gray, stay here. You're in charge."

"You're not going without me!" No way was I going to stay behind when I knew it had something to do with—"It's about Chav, isn't it?

He's run off, right?" I got between her and the door so she couldn't get past me. "I'm going with you."

"Gray, you can't! He took Christopher's gun."

That shocked me silly for a minute. I stood there.

"Lock all the doors and pull the curtains. I've got to go see if I can do anything." Liana headed past me, but I grabbed her by the arm. I'm as big as she is, bigger actually, and I'm a lot younger. If it came to a wrestling match, I doubted she could make me stay behind.

But I didn't have to fight her. I'm pretty good at arguing. "If he has a gun, what makes you think we're safe here by ourselves?" I pointed out. Not that I ever for a minute thought Chav would hurt any of us. But Aunt Lee was a parent, so she had to be scared of everything. It was in her job description.

"Damn, you're right," she muttered. "Okay, come on, all three of you. Hurry."

Baval and Chavali were standing there in their slippers and pj's, hanging on to each other like the roof of their lives was caving in. Probably that's how they felt. Chav had always been the solidest thing in the world to them. I threw coats around them and herded them to the car before Lee could change her mind.

They huddled together like puppies in the back-seat while Lee tried out areas of her speedometer she'd never used before. All the way out to the stable the only thing she said was, "He hit Chris on the head and took the gun."

It must have been the rifle Topher had been keeping in the corner of the stable. I asked, "Did he take Rom?"

Liana just lifted one hand like she didn't know.

There were two cop cars parked in the stable yard, their blue flashing lights looking chilly even in the sunshine. Topher was okay—I saw him first thing, standing there holding an ice pack to the back of his head. The second thing I saw was Grandpa, facing off with him.

". . . withholding evidence!" Grandpa was yelling at Topher as we got out of the car. "That's a crime, but what's worse is if you'd told me about the goddamn horse, I would have taken the boy in, this wouldn't have happened."

Topher said in that quiet way of his, "You don't know for sure what might have happened."

"What the hell are you trying to say?"

"I'm saying it could have been worse. The boy is desperate. I didn't want him cornered."

"You didn't want!"

"I handled it the best way I could." Topher wasn't shouting, but he wouldn't step back and he wouldn't give in. Grandpa was all but screaming.

"You got no goddamn business handling it at all! I'd slap the cuffs on you, but I don't trust myself to do it without punching you in the nose. I take this personal. My daughter's involved."

"What that kid's going through is everybody's business," Topher said, real low. "And I know your daughter's involved. When this is over I have every intention of marrying your daughter if she'll have me. So I take this personal too."

That surprised Grandpa quiet for a minute. And standing there, holding Baval and Chavali by their hands, Liana just sort of gasped. Topher turned and saw her, and his face went pink. They stared at each other.

I didn't get to see how it turned out, because I was heading into the stable. Let the adults stand around making hot air. I knew what I had to do. Somebody had to find Chav.

"Thank God." There stood Rom, gazing at me over his stall door with eyes deep as midnight. I was sure Chav would not have taken any other horse. He was afoot, and that meant there was a chance I could catch up to him.

Quietly I got Rom out of his stall and put a bridle on him—just a bridle, there was no time for a saddle. I vaulted onto his shining black back right there in the barn, where nobody would see me in time to stop me.

This was one time I wasn't riding fat furry little Paradiddle. If I was going to find Chav, it had to be like in the poem, it had to be on the galloping black stallion, Rom, shining like black fire even in the shadows of the barn.

I felt different on Rom, like I could do anything. The Barb stallion was not tall, yet being on him felt immense.

Chav was out there somewhere carrying a gun.

Turning Rom toward the door, I whispered to his pricked black ears, "Please, we've got to find him before he does something crazy." I'm not saying he understood. But he knew something was going on. He was quivering all over. When I tightened my legs he bunched to run. Yet his mouth listened to my grip on the reins.

I leaned forward, grabbed hold of his long mane, and let him go.

He plunged that heavy head of his and leaped into a dead run within a stride. It was like riding a thunderbolt, a streak of black lightning, the wind before a storm. I heard people yell—Topher, Grandpa, Lee—but never really saw them. By the time I blinked they were left behind, we were sweeping across the countryside.

Empty countryside. Where had Chav gone?

We were out of sight of the stable now. Every inch of me ached from the force of the black horse's galloping. I slowed Rom to a jog and tried to think, tried to imagine myself inside Chav's mind. Where would he have gone?

My life is the color of midnight.
The black horse of anger gallops closer. . . .
The world will die under his iron tread,
And the moon in my sky is a cold dead eye . . .

I had to face it: Chav was hurting enough to want
to die. And angry enough to want to kill.

CHAPTER

—11—

Sitting in Topher's passenger seat, on his way out to the stable, Chav felt something inside him come apart—he could almost hear it snap, like a bone breaking, only it was not a bone, it was—him. He said nothing but knew: it would soon be over. Any personal togetherness he had managed to maintain was going fast since Baval and Chavali no longer needed him. He felt like two or more people now.

Show them, one of him said. Kill them all.

Not this one too, begged the other. Not Topher.

Yes, Topher too, you wuss, you coward, you little bloody-nose crybaby, can't you do anything right? No wonder you always ended up on the floor, no wonder you could never win. You're no good. You're a loser.

Shut up. Let me alone. I just want to die.

It was as if time had skipped a few beats. Next

thing he was there, walking into the stable, and Rom whinnied and nodded his long strong head out the stall door, glad to see him. "Hi, Gypsy horse," he whispered, rubbing Rom's forehead, laying his cheek against the flannel softness of the horse's nose. It seemed to be okay to love animals. And there was no need to be afraid of Rom any longer. No need any longer to be afraid of the black stallion of anger. Whatever had to happen was going to happen.

Briefly Chav regretted not being able to give the horse to Gray. She would have liked that.

Shut up about Gray. She's just another god-damn gadjo. Kill them all.

No, not all.

All! Kill them. It's the only way a pansy like you will ever be somebody.

Topher came in with the grooming box. "Gotta get him shined up for tonight," he muttered.

Rom shone already like the death angel's black wings. Topher had been feeding him well. Brushing him. Taking good care of him.

When Topher put the grooming box down and bent over it, Chav reached for a broom handle and hit him with it, hard, on the back of the head.

Topher fell and lay still.

As if he had been rehearsing this all his life Chav walked over to the corner where the rifle stood, where he had seen it the day he brought Rom here. Yes, it was still there. He checked it—

127

yes, it was loaded. He cradled it and took two boxes of ammunition from the wall joist above it.

Turned, and knew he should start by killing Topher.

No.

Yes. He's a stinking gadjo.

No. He loves horses.

To bloody red hell with love! What has love ever done for you? Made you a flattened worm, that's what. Kill him. Kill them all, or—

Okay, okay! In a minute.

First he pulled the note out of his jacket pocket and dropped it in the middle of the dirt floor. Then he picked it up and reread it. He had written and rewritten the note in the dark morning hours of the night before, after Gray and the others had gone back to bed. It said:

> *Dear Gray and Lee,*
> *As you will know by the time you read this, I am no good. Baval and Chavali are nice kids, but you don't want me. I know you will take good care of them, so now I can go. Please get Baval to a doctor. He saw too many awful things when he was little—our darling father used to make him watch. He can't bear it, so he shut it all out of his mind, he doesn't remember anything that happened before we ran away. He doesn't really remember Mom or any-*

thing, and all those stories I told him made it worse. I'm scared someday it will all come back and make him crazy like me. Maybe a doctor can help him.

I hope Chavali will be okay. She doesn't remember much either, but it's just because she was so little.

Just as a safeguard so nobody can ever send them back to their father, please don't try to find out their real names. I am going because I am bad clear through like him, I am full of hate like him. I don't want to hurt Baval and Chavali, but I don't care about anybody else. So you can just forget about me.

Love,
Chav

You total jerkhead, can't you do anything right? You signed it "Love"!

There had to be a pen someplace. He could scribble it out.

On the floor Topher stirred and groaned.

No time to scribble it out, unless he killed Topher right now . . .

No.

There was no time to argue with himself, either. *Just drop the damn note and take the horse and get out of here.*

He laid the note near Topher's limp hand. Rom

looked down at him with wise, calm, midnight-dark eyes.

Rom was not the black stallion of his rage.

"No," Chav said aloud to him, "you stay behind. No more Gypsy scum for you. Go to the rich gadjo farm and be happy and make many foals with many mares." Then he was suddenly furious. "Stop looking at me!" he screamed, and he ran.

His feet hurt, as always, because more than once his father had broken them. All his life they had hurt, and all his life they would keep on hurting.

All his life? Not too much longer now.

At the ruined cemetery he stopped running and sat on the white back of the broken angel with a rifle in his hand. He panted awhile and thought. One thing he was right about: Rom. Even though he had left Rom behind, the black stallion of anger was still with him, galloping, galloping in his chest.

"They think I did this," Chav muttered, looking around at the toppled markers, the torn-up graves. "I will give them more to bury here. They can bury me here too if they like. But I know they will not like."

When he got up he knew where he was going. It was Saturday afternoon. The big game was going on. Matt Kain and Fishy Fischel and all their gadjo buddies would be there. And a few thousand gadjos more.

Chav cradled the rifle like a baby and walked. Every few steps something made him hurt, maybe his feet, maybe a thought, maybe his heart aching, and he cursed. Most of the leaves had fallen. From beyond the brown hills ahead of him floated the booming of the band.

*　　*　　*

I whispered to the black stallion, "Where would he go, Rom? We have to find him." But I didn't know how it was going to happen. I couldn't track him. Chav wasn't a horse, he didn't leave much of a trail, and anyway it hadn't rained in over a week now. The ground was hard again.

Rom's ears flicked back toward me, listening to me. I loosened the reins. "Which way, boy?"

At a smooth floating trot he headed toward the railroad tracks.

"Where is Chav?" I kept asking him or the air or maybe myself. "Where is Chav?"

It was weird. I'm still not sure what was going on, whether Rom actually understood what was happening, or whether he was tracking Chav by scent, or whether riding Chav's black stallion of anger gave me enough insight to head me in the right direction, along the tracks toward town. Sometimes Rom chose which way we went, and sometimes I did, or maybe we both did. We were joined, like two parts of the same black animal. I even had on my black jeans that day, and I felt black hooves pounding hard and hurtfully in my chest.

"He is so angry," I whispered. "When they beat you and beat you and beat you, it makes you feel like roadkill, like you are almost nothing, and it makes you feel like you have to hit back or die."

Or maybe it was just stupid luck leading Rom and me. We checked the "castle," the silo—it was empty. We circled through the woods. When we came back to the tracks again, there was Chav.

There he was at the far end of the railroad bridge, aiming the gun straight at me.

I pulled Rom to a halt and sat there, and I think every part of me started to sweat at once. I don't know which scared me more, the idea of getting shot by Chav—though I never really thought Chav would shoot me—or the idea of crossing that damn high bridge over that damn deep water to get to him. I was riding bareback, and being on Rom was not like riding Diddle. Rom snorted and surged even when he walked. If Rom decided to dance in the middle of the trestle, I might fly off and land sixty feet below, in the river.

Sixty-eight feet, counting being eight feet up above the bridge on the horse.

"Stay away!" Chav yelled. Floating to me across the river, his voice sounded like Baval's did some-times: high and shaky. He was just a kid, really, and he was as scared as I was.

That settled it somehow. I gathered the reins

for control, squeezed Rom gently with my knees, and started him forward.

"No! Go away!" Chav sounded panicky.

"I can't," I called. This was really true, because the horse was on the bridge now. No way I was going to try to turn him around on that narrow, dangerous slab of concrete.

"Stop! Don't come any closer!"

I kept going. Sure, I was scared, but I had to do it. I had to get to Chav.

"Stop where you are, or I'll shoot!"

"No, you won't." If he did, and I fell in the river, I'd never live . . . but I felt pretty sure he wouldn't, and even more sure he wouldn't risk hurting Rom.

"I will! I'll shoot! You're a gadjo."

Suddenly I was mad. "Gadjo, schmadjo!" I shouted at him so loud Rom flinched. "That's just something you made up so you could hate everybody!"

I was close enough now to really see his face, and it hurt to look at. All the pain and rage he had ever hidden from me were glaring out of his eyes.

"Damn you, Gray!" The gun barrel shook in his hands like a branch in the wind. He backed away from me. "Okay, goddamn you, I can't do it, I can't hurt you, but I can still hurt the others. You stay away."

"What others?" I had Rom off the bridge now, finally. It was easier to breathe and easier to concentrate on talking to Chav.

"Kain. Fischel. All their sucky friends. All the pissy people in your gadjo school. In your gadjo town. They'll all be there, won't they? At your big important homecoming game for people who actually have a home?"

My God. I had to stop him, I had to get that gun away from him somehow.

I could have charged him with Rom, I guess. Knocked him down. But would Rom do it? Could I make him do it, and could I get the gun without hurting Chav or the horse? It was risky. I took a different sort of chance instead—I slipped down off Rom. It didn't feel right to be looking down on Chav, to be talking at him from above.

"You're heading for the game to kill people?" I tried not to sound too horrified, because then he would think it was him making me sick, and it wasn't. What he was thinking of doing was awful, but Chav was not a bad person. Even though he probably thought he was.

"Them, and me. Take as many as I can with me, then off myself." He kept the gun up to his shoulder, and talked loud and fast, and his eyes were wild as a spooked mustang's.

"What if Liana were there?" Even though I knew he knew she wasn't.

"Then I would go someplace else. McDonald's or someplace. I could never hurt you or Liana." He calmed down some just saying her name. "But—"

I let loose. "But you think what you're going to do won't hurt me?" I yelled at him. "You think if other kids die, I won't cry? Chav, people are people! There's no such thing as gadjo or Gypsy. Anything that hurts anybody hurts me!"

He was gawking at me but not like he understood. I wasn't explaining very well, but I had to keep talking.

I said, "What if Minda's there?" My voice shook, because it was true, she might be. Then I couldn't talk, even if I thought of something else to say, which I didn't. I stood there staring at him, watching the struggle go on in him. He stood in the middle of the railroad tracks with his face stone hard and his eyes like a black cloudy night.

Then his hard face seemed to break, and he let the gun sag. "Okay," he burst out, "okay, screw it. You don't want me to, I won't."

"Chav," I whispered, and I reached out toward him to thank him, but he jumped back.

"I'll just—get rid of me." His voice was going to pieces. "That's the main—point, anyway. End it." He stepped back more, still on the tracks but way out of my reach, and turned the rifle so that the barrel tip rested under his nose and his thumb was on the trigger.

"No!" Oh my God, no, he couldn't. "Chav, why not just kill me too!" I cried at him. "You do this, I'll die inside anyway. I'll hurt every time I think of you."

135

His hand shook and pulled away from the trigger. I saw that, but mainly I watched his face. His mouth, stretched tight and trembling. His eyes, staring at me, black with pain, like a trapped animal's.

I made myself be quiet and calm. "Why?" I asked him gently. "Why do you want to do this? Tell me."

"I—need to die."

"Because you want to hurt somebody?"

"Because I—I'm—*hateful.*"

His hand started toward the trigger again. He was really going to do it and I couldn't stop him, my heart could break right there and make a bright red puddle on the railroad tracks and it wouldn't stop him. I could only think of one thing that might stop him. "Carl!" I screamed at him. "Your mother, tell me! Why did she die?"

I had to do it, I had to get through to him somehow, but his face twisted like I'd knifed him. "Don't!" he screamed back at me. "Don't talk about her!"

"We've got to. Did she kill herself? Tell me!"

"*No!* It was my father, he—beat—"

He closed his eyes in agony, and tears ran down his scarred face.

"He beat her and beat her, we were all hiding under the table and he banged her head against the floor—"

I went to him and pushed the gun aside and put my arms around him.

136

He was crying so hard he could barely talk, or I could barely understand. I only caught a few words now and then—"blood got all over me"—I hugged him and led him off the tracks to a patch of grass and got him to sit down—"dead, but—in the morning she was just gone"—I sat with him and held him—"like he put her out with the garbage. No funeral, no flowers"—Chav stopped trying to talk. I cradled him against my shoulder, and Rom came over and nosed him, and he cried—every sob should have ended the world. I had never heard anyone cry that way, not even Liana the day everyone died, not even me.

I sat and held him, and Rom stood there with his reins hanging, peering down at both of us, and the earth and sky stayed together, though I felt as if they should fall apart. After a while I reached down and tried to slip the rifle away from him, which was a mistake. He hung on to it, and sat up, pulling away from me.

"Chav," I said to him softly, "I've lost one brother. Don't make me lose another one. Please."

He looked at me, wet-eyed. "Is that—what I am?" he asked, his voice thick with crying. "Your brother?"

"Yes."

His shoulders relaxed, and he laid his head back against my neck, and one of his arms came up to hug me.

He cried all the rest of the afternoon. It was like being in a thunderstorm—he couldn't make it stop. Once he got up and staggered into the woods to vomit from crying so much. He'd finally let go of the rifle, he'd left it behind, and I grabbed it and ran a few steps onto the bridge and flung it into the river. Chav came back and didn't seem to notice. He just sank down in the grass with the sobs still shaking him, and I went to him and held him again, and he let me.

By the time the sun was going down he was so exhausted he could look me in the eye and tell me things he never could have said before. He lay on the grass facing up at me and told me how his father had once tied him to a tree and left him there for two days as a punishment. How his father had once locked him in the basement for a week. How no one in the family was allowed to use the telephone or bring friends home and no one was ever allowed to help him, not his brother, not even his mother. How she never fought back— sometimes he had hated her for not fighting back. Then he had hated himself and decided he must deserve it when his father hurt him.

"It was always Mom or me he went after," he said, terribly calm now, terribly tired—he was finally done crying. "He never hit Robbie, but sometimes he made him watch. In a way, that might have been worse."

It took me a minute to catch on. "Robbie is Baval?"

"Yes. But don't say it to him, he doesn't remember. Someday Dad is going to come at him out of a bad dream. . . ." Chav closed his eyes. "I hate Robbie sometimes too."

"But you love him at the same time."

"I—that's what hurts, the love. Dad—now I hate him, but then—I kept trying and trying to please him—I wanted—I just wanted him to—smile at me. . . ."

He couldn't quite say that he had wanted his father to love him. For a while he lay with his eyes closed. I reached over and stroked his hair back from his forehead.

"Let's get you home," I said.

He didn't open his eyes. "Gray—it hurts so bad, I don't know if I'm going to make it."

I knew he wasn't talking about just getting home, because I remembered the feeling from a couple of years before. "You'll make it," I told him. He had to. "Come on. Are you ready to ride?"

He opened his eyes and looked up at the horse standing over him very black in the gray dusk. Then he stood up, wobbly on his feet, and leaned against Rom, his face against the stallion's strong arched neck, hidden in mane. I knew: Once a small hurt boy had run to his mother like that, pressing his cheek against her long black hair.

"This big guy isn't the black horse I was scared of," Chav muttered. "All that crap is inside me."

Then he straightened, and his eyes were clear, and I really began to hope for him, because I didn't see much anger in him anymore, just a terrible sadness that I knew would pass.

I vaulted onto Rom first, because Chav was still pretty shaky. I helped him up behind me, and he leaned on me, laying his head against the back of my neck. We had to go across the railroad bridge in the almost-dark, but I trusted Rom and didn't let myself be scared. I couldn't. Somebody had to take care of Chav.

CHAPTER

—12—

It was nightfall by the time we got back over the cemetery hill, but Topher had the floodlights on, and it looked like half the world was there at the stable, including the big Spanish Dancer Ranch horse trailer that had come for Fuerza Epica.

"Chav," I said, and I felt his head come up to look, and I felt his hands grip at my shoulders when he saw.

"You feeling okay to take it from here?" I asked, because I thought it might be good if he did.

He didn't answer, and I felt his hands shake a little but not too bad. Maybe they just needed to get back on the reins.

I halted Rom, swung my leg over his neck, and slipped down. "All yours," I told Chav. "Show them what the black horse can do."

He had a choice, then: he could show them the black horse of anger galloping through the night, or he could show them Rom. From the way I had seen him ride I figured he knew what Rom could do. I stood aside and waited.

Without looking at me he gathered the double reins into his hands like an expert, collected the Barb stallion, and eased him into a slow, graceful walk down the hill toward where the cop cars and reporters and gawkers waited along with maybe a few people who actually cared.

Everybody saw him when he reached the level. About three dozen voices shouted, and some people started toward him and some ducked back as if he still had a gun. But then they all stopped where they were and watched, because Chav had given a signal and the black Barb stallion was dancing.

Diagonally at an airy trot he danced toward them. Then Chav lifted him into a canter so slow and floating it was like a waltz, it circled and swirled—Chav signaled Rom for a change of direction at each stride. Rom's reaching forelegs curved and turned like a ballet dancer's reaching arms, like a dream, yet he was made of power, dynamite in the darkness, his barrel and shoulders and that thick arched neck so black they shone fiery white. People could not stop watching him. I walked up to stand with the rest of the crowd, and it was as still as church, and no one noticed me, they were watching so hard.

It might have been three or four minutes. I

don't know. Time didn't seem to count anymore. When Chav put Rom through one last long trotting diagonal and rode him up to the stable yard, everyone blinked and looked around like they'd forgotten where they were.

Standing with Topher was a straight, handsome white-haired woman in a white blouse and wrap skirt. Chav halted Rom in front of her, put one hand down by his side, and lowered his head in a formal bow. Saluting the judge, I think they call it. The way he must have felt, the world was there to judge him that night.

Then he slipped down off Rom, handed over the reins, and turned away.

But the woman stopped him with a touch. "I know you."

Chav faced her, wild-eyed, scared. Baval and Chavali had come running out of somewhere and grabbed him, hanging on his waist, and his hands spread out and down, one over each of them to protect them.

"I've seen you ride," the white-haired woman said. "You took second in a show at—"

"Please," Chav whispered. "Nobody here knows my real name."

The woman nodded as if she understood. "And then because you had not gotten first place, your father took you behind the grandstand and hit you across the face with the butt of a crop." Her voice had gone low. "I saw it, I reported it, but no one would do anything. He is a very rich, very power-ful man."

Baval's head had come up. He was listening with a frozen, thinking look on his face.

Chav begged the woman, "I can't let him find out where we are."

"Confound it, Chav!" Grandpa was there with his jaw sticking out. "You think we'd let anything happen to you or your brother or sister? That son of a bitch is not going to get near you without walking over top of me. And you can't let him get away with what he did to you. He belongs in jail."

"He killed our mother," Baval whispered.

"What?" Grandpa exclaimed, gawking at him.

"He killed Mom. I saw it happen." Baval held on hard to Chav, and the look on his face—I tried to get to him, but somebody, Minda, had grabbed me, was jumping up and down and hugging me. And Lee was there, asking again and again if I was okay.

Chav was not okay. Staring at a policeman, he didn't seem to understand much that was happening around him. "You need to put me in jail," he said straight to Grandpa. "I was crazy. I wanted to kill people."

"We don't put kids in jail."

"You've got to!" Chav struggled a step closer to him. "I wrecked the graveyard, right? Put me in jail."

"That's not true!" Minda finally let go of me to run over to Grandpa. "That's not true. I know who trashed the cemetery, and it wasn't Chav. It was—"

"Not right now," I told her. I'd finally managed to go over there myself and get hold of Baval, and I could feel him shaking. "Grandpa, please do something."

Grandpa was saying to Minda, "I already heard. The Fischel boy and his friends. Fishy talked to Peck and me this afternoon. Peck's pretty broken up about it. His own son, for God's sake."

Liana said sharply, "Dad, are you done with Chav? Baval looks sick. We've got to get them out of here."

"I hit Topher," Chav insisted. "That's assault with a deadly weapon, right?"

"Heck, I been hurt worse by a pony foal," Topher said.

"I stole Rom!"

Apparently this had already been discussed. With her hand on Rom's neck, the white-haired woman was shaking her head and smiling. Grandpa said a little peevishly, "Chav, I'm sorry, but I can't seem to make anything stick. Nobody wants to press charges against you."

Shaking in my arms, Baval started to moan. Chav looked down, and his eyes widened. "Bro, what's the matter? What's wrong?"

"Dad killed Mom," Baval whispered, moaning. "He was too big, and he hit her too hard, and her head came open. There was so much blood she has to be dead. There was so much blood she has to be dead. There was so much blood she has to be—"

"Oh my God." Chav grabbed Baval and hugged him against his chest. Over his brother's head he looked hollow-eyed at me.

"—dead. There was so much blood—"

It was awful to listen to Baval chanting it over and over, his mind caught on a memory he couldn't bear. "We better get that kid to a hospital," Grandpa said. "Chav, is it true what he says? Your father killed your mother?"

I guess Chav had had too much. He cried out at Grandpa, "Don't talk to me about him! I'm just like him!"

"No, you're not," Grandpa told him gently. "You just need a little help sorting things out, and that's what doctors are for. Come on, both of you."

"—so much blood, she has to be dead—"

Grandpa and Liana got Chav and Baval in the cruiser and drove out. I heard later they went straight to the hospital. Topher helped the Spanish Dancer Ranch woman load Rom onto the trailer, all wrapped and rugged to travel, the shining blackness of him all covered over. I saw one flash of a midnight eye, and then the doors closed, the truck rolled away, and the black stallion was gone. And even though there were still people chattering everywhere, even though Chavali was hanging on to my hand, I stood there feeling all alone.

*   *   *

Chav and Baval were both in the hospital for a few days. It was hard on Chavali.

"Where's Rom?" she asked me at bedtime that first night.

I was dead tired from everything that had happened. "In the big trailer," I told her, "going home." *Where's Chav? In a strange room, in the dark, with bars on the windows, probably, and a nurse sticking a needle into him.*

Chavali sat up, cozy in her own bed and her pink pj's. "What will happen then?" she asked me anxiously, and I began to see: She needed a story.

Okay. I could do this, as long as it was about horses.

"The horses will all come out to meet him," I said slowly, making it up as I went along. "It is a big beautiful farm with big trees and white fences and lots of horses, all kinds, Arabians and Andalusians and warm-bloods and mustangs and, uh, medicine hat pintos and little fat ponies. They all line up and wait to see Rom again, because he is their prince. See, his real name is Epic Fire, which means way, way back his great-great-great-great grandfather was a fire horse, but Rom didn't know that because he was stolen away when he was a baby. His father is the king of all dancing horses—"

"What's a fire horse?" Chavali demanded.

Really I guess it was a horse that pulled a fire engine, but now I was getting into this. "It's a horse who's a son of the sun," I said. "See, the sun horse gallops across the sky and he's all fire. But his colts and fillies came to earth and they just had manes and tails made of fire."

"And wings," Chavali suggested.

"Okay, yeah, wings made of fire. And their colts and fillies didn't have the wings anymore. And *their* colts and fillies just had regular manes and tails with a fire forelock. And so on, until finally the fire horses just look like regular horses, but they still have sun fire inside. Rom is one of those. That's why he's a prince."

"Will the horses bow when he comes home?" Chavali asked. "Will all the different kinds of horses bow to him because he's a prince?"

I thought about that and decided against it. "No, it's more like they're very, very glad to see him, because they love him. They'll nuzzle him and kiss him. His father the king will put a crown on him." This story was starting to sound awfully familiar. "They'll order in a truckload of pizza and have a feast."

Chavali started to giggle. "Horses don't eat pizza!"

"Maybe they'd like to, but nobody ever gives them any. They eat bread, and they eat tomatoes, so why wouldn't they eat pizza?"

"They wouldn't eat pepperoni!"

"They could order plain."

Chavali was laughing, which was good. I got up and kissed her and told her g'night, but she got serious again.

"Does Rom like pizza, really?"

"He just absolutely loves pizza."

"So he's happy? He likes being back with his father the king?"

"Yes. He's happy."

"And his father likes him?"

"His father loves him."

Chavali lay down, but I could see she was thinking of more questions.

"Is his father a black stallion too?"

I decided to leave it up to her. "I don't know. What color do you want his father to be?"

She thought for a long time. Then, "We'll call and ask," she said firmly.

"Okay."

"Can we call Chav tomorrow?"

"Yes." We would whether we could or not.

"And Baval?"

"Yes."

"Will Chav be home soon?"

"I hope."

* * *

Chav came home first, after three days, Tuesday evening. Grandpa brought him home. For some reason Grandpa was starting to like him and Baval and Chavali. I didn't understand it back then, but the way to get Grandpa to like you is to stand up to him. He didn't appreciate it much at first, but after a while he really respected the way Liana and Topher and I stood up for Chav, and he liked the way Chav wouldn't tell him anything. Now he wanted the kids to stay as much as Lee and I did. He wasn't mad at me anymore.

Chavali and I had been busy making some preparations. And Liana too. We had everything ready when Chav came in the door.

He acted tired and shy. "Hi," he said without really looking at anybody. Then he glanced over and saw Topher sitting on the sofa. "Uh, how's your head?" Topher had not been allowed to visit him in the hospital, just Lee and Grandpa.

"Better," Topher told him.

"I'm really sorry."

"You're sorry it's better?" Topher was trying to make him smile. It didn't work.

"Sorry for what I did."

"Son, don't give it another thought," Topher told him gently. "Just work on getting well."

"That's what I've got to do. The doctors say the bad feelings will get easier for me to handle.

They say if I talk to people, keep seeing my thera-pist . . ." Chav let the words fade away. He didn't sound as if he really believed any of this.

"Chav," I said to him.

"Hey, Gray." He made himself look at me. "Thanks for what you did."

"Quit it with the thankses and the sorries, turkey." I grinned at him. "Tell me something. What do you smell?"

His head came up as he sniffed the air, and the forelock swished back from his eyes, and for a moment I saw the black stallion in him again. He said, "Pizza."

"How much?" I challenged him.

"Huh?"

He didn't get it yet. "Tons and tons of pizza," Liana told him, rolling her eyes. I had coached her on what to say. "Gray put in an order for a *truck-load* of pizza. We're going to have to drag people in off the streets, or else be eating pizza for days."

"A truck—" The word caught in Chav's throat. His eyes went wide.

I nodded at Topher, and he stood up and pulled it out of his pocket, the headband, the one Chavali and I had been working on, made of play money coins fastened together. It had taken us a while to get it the way we wanted it, but finally it turned out really beautiful, almost like a crown. "Son," Topher said to Chav, holding it out, "I

151

understand that Liana and I are supposed to give you this."

Chav stared. He couldn't seem to move or breathe.

"It goes on him, silly," Liana told Topher, and she took it and slipped it gently into place on Chav's head. Against his black hair it shone like real gold.

Tears started down his face.

"Chav?" Lee hugged him, and he hung on to her like a baby. Then Topher was hugging him too, and Grandpa looked worried, but I could tell it was all right. These were the good kind of tears, the warm kind, not the kind that had cut him open like knives that afternoon beside the railroad tracks.

"Pizza feast time!" I hollered.

Chav looked at me, his face wet. "Gray," he said, "I just absolutely hate you," meaning the opposite.

"Chavali helped," I told him.

"C'mere, sis." He got down on his knees, and she ran to him, and he gathered her close to his heart.

"I wish Baval was here," she told him.

"So do I." He kept hold of her. "But he's gonna be okay. We talked a lot. He's gonna be fine. He'll be home in a few days."

She pulled back enough to look at him kneeling there with the plastic-money crown on his head.

"Chav," she asked him, "is there really such a thing as a prince?"

He hesitated.

"I think there is," Liana said. "A prince doesn't have to be perfect. I think you're looking at one."

CHAPTER

—13—

Journal   **Mrs. Higby**
April 17   **Language Arts**
Chav Calderone

Gray's birthday present is done, finally. Chris got me all different colors of horsehair, red and yellow and black and white and gray, and I braided her a five-color bracelet the way my mother used to do it. And I'm putting my new poem in the box. It doesn't seem like enough after everything, but it's the best I can do. I know she'll love it.

I'll make Chavali a bracelet when I get a chance, and Liana. I wish she and Chris would just go ahead and get married instead of waiting until the addition on his house gets done. I mean, I wouldn't mind sleeping on a sofa awhile. It's not like I need to have a bedroom to myself. I'm so lucky just to have a family I can't believe it. Lately I'm feeling a lot better about everything. I mean, I know I've got a long way to go, and a lot of the time I still slip up and think the way my father beat into me, but I feel like I can change that. I can do things. I'm not even scared of testifying against my father anymore—at least not much, not when Mr. Calderone is on my side—I think he'd pull out that cop gun of his and shoot anybody who tried to hurt me or take me away from here.

It's a good thing I finally got the guts to tell him my father's name, considering that my father had hired goons to look for us kids. I can't believe I thought we were safe. Mr. Calderone is right, the son of a bitch belongs in jail. Daddy dear could hire his hit men and lie to everybody and say we kids were going to school in Europe, but he couldn't lie about where Mom was once the cops got a warrant and found the body. He's finally going to pay, and it feels kind of good.

And kind of bad. Okay, I am scared, some. I'll be glad when it's over. But it's the right thing to do.

Baval says he'll testify too, but I don't want him to. He's still real shaky inside.

155

The doctors say stop blaming myself for everything, it's not because of all the stories I told him. They say actually they were good, they were what he needed at the time. And Liana says they were not lies, stories don't have to be fact to be true. Some days I even kind of understand that.

Life is amazing. It's better than any story I could make up. Of all the wild and crazy things, now Mr. Fischel doesn't seem to mind anymore that I'm part Gypsy. He says hi when I ride by.

What's even wilder, Minda is going with Fishy. After she found out he and his friends got drunk and wrecked the cemetery, after she talked with him and made him tell his father, now he likes her. He even treats her right. I guess maybe he never really talked with a girl before.

I wonder why Gray doesn't think she's ever going to have a boyfriend. I'm glad, because the whole idea of that kind of love scares me silly, after what my dad did to my mom. And I want to keep her as my sister forever. But I want her to be happy, so I just wonder—

Never mind, time's up. Gotta go dissect some poor dead poem. That's okay. Even Mrs. Higby doesn't seem so bad these days.

＊　　＊　　＊

Things happened. I turned fourteen; I wore the horsehair bracelet Chav gave me almost every day; Liana and Chris got married, so she is a Worthwine; and they started proceedings to get legal custody of Chav and Baval and Chavali, and then adopt all us kids, but I won't have to change my name. I am still Gray Calderone and Chav is a Calderone too. He says he just likes the name, but I think maybe it is more like I adopted him first. I think that because of the poem he gave me. It says:

> *I came here Prince of Scars*
> *King of Hunger*
> *Lord of Anger*
> *on a black horse riding*
> *in the dark of midnight*
> *in the dark of my heart*
> *in fear*
> *but here*
> *you made me Prince of Pizza*
> *King of Calderone*
> *Lord of Topher*
> *by a Gray girl riding*
> *in the daylight of my heart*
> *with a crown of happiness*
> *You brought me home*

You better believe I am going to keep that poem forever.

More things that happened: we moved out to the stable. The Spanish Dancer Ranch sent Chav a poster of Rom, I mean Fuerza Epica, and an invitation to come ride for them someday. Minda bought a boy gerbil that performed a miracle and had babies. Baval and Chavali each got one. I helped Chris retrain Red the white Thoroughbred, and so did Chav. Chavali got a fat little dapple-dun pony. Baval started riding Dude sometimes, since Minda wasn't riding as much anymore. I decided what Dude's color was: palominto. Get it? Palomino pinto.

It's funny how some things work out. You give away a lunch or two, and look what happens.

There was a day that first summer when Chav and I went riding up the hill past the Fischel cemetery and out along the tracks to the abandoned Altland farm. I looked at him sometimes while we rode, because he was beautiful to look at the way he sat a horse. He wore his black jeans but a white T-shirt—he did that sometimes those days, wore white or silver or gray as well as black. I figured someday he'd surprise me and graduate to real colors.

We didn't talk much. Chav was riding Red, only he called her Angel—she was his horse now. He had to concentrate on keeping her together. She took a good rider because on the trail she was frightened of everything, but that what he was, a good rider, because he had a feeling about

158

horses. He never seemed to get angry at Angel. At other things, plenty, including at me sometimes, but never at Angel.

Me? I rode Paradiddle. I guess I really did have a horse of my own now; in fact, I had a couple dozen. I could ride any horse on the place, and I rode them all one time or another, but for some reason I kept coming back to Diddle, blimpy middle and curly hair and all. Chav and I were just taking a quiet ride, not trying to prove anything to anybody, so I rode Diddle.

Nothing had changed at the Altland place except that the grass and wildflowers were tall in the meadow now. We rode down the slope to the empty silo and halted the horses and just sat there looking.

"It hasn't even been a year," Chav said.

"Seems so long," I teased him. It did, but only because it felt like he'd always been my brother.

He barely smiled. It took a lot to make him smile. "Seems so different," he said. "Everything's changed. Back then I didn't . . ." He went silent, looking around like something might sneak up on him. By then, living with him, I had learned to keep my big mouth shut sometimes. I sat and listened to Diddle swishing her tail and waited.

He said, "Back then I didn't ever think I'd keep, you know, living. I felt like a Kleenex or something: use it and then throw it away. Baval and

Chavali were the ones who counted, not me. I felt thin as paper."

I waited some more.

Chav said, "Nowadays this whole idea that I'm going to have a life, I can be something, maybe a horse trainer, maybe a poet or a songwriter or a storyteller—it feels so strange. I mean, it feels great, but really, really strange. I can't believe it. I still can't believe I'm going to be okay."

"You're gonna be okay," I told him.

"Doofus, I just said that."

"But you don't believe it."

"Give me a break. What about you, Gray? Are you going to make it?"

"Huh?"

Over Angel's pricked white ears he looked straight at me and said, "Tell me about the accident."

He wasn't asking for information—he had heard all about it from Liana and Grandma and Grandpa. There was a hard edge in his voice. He was challenging me.

Oh no. I could fool all the adults, but I couldn't fool Chav. He saw right through me, how I wasn't handling it as well as I pretended. The others saw me smiling in the daytime; they didn't suspect how I still cried at night sometimes. But Chav knew. Not that he had heard me or anything—he just knew.

"Chav—"

"Gray, you are going to do this. Tell me about the accident."

"Damn it, Chav!" I yelled hard enough to make Diddle jump. "Who the hell do you think you are?"

"Your brother. I am doing this because I loathe you and detest you and this is my way of showing it." His voice was gentle now. "C'mon."

I knew who he was. He was a boy who had mothered his sister and brother for a year and a half on his own. He was a kid who had come apart and put himself back together in a new and better way. He had been on the ground and still had his eyes on the sky. He was Chav. So I told him.

"Uncle Dan had this boat . . ." I started over because I wasn't telling it very well. "He had a big boat, and he had a cottage on Lake Champlain, which is, you know, a really huge lake. We were all supposed to go up for a weekend, but I got sick. I had the flu. So Lee said she'd stay with me, and everybody else should go. She never liked boating all that much, but the rest of us loved it. Including me. I was so mad that I had to go and get sick."

My voice started to shake, but Chav nodded to me to keep me going. His eyes were quiet and soft and steady on me.

"So it was a hot sunny day, and they were all out in the middle of the lake, and they all jumped in to swim. All of them, even little Carrie and Cassie." No, I couldn't do this after all. My voice was shaking too bad, and I had to hide my face.

"Gray, don't stop." I felt Chav's hand on my shoulder, warm, bridging the distance between us. "Keep going. You have to talk about it. You've got to."

I had made him do things sometimes. He was maybe the one person in the world who had a right to make me do this. So I blurted it out. "They—it was so stupid, they couldn't get back in the boat! It was too high. . . ." Never mind what my face was showing—I looked at him. "See, usually Liana would have been there to give them a hand back in, because she doesn't like to swim. It just so happened we'd never gone in all at once before, so nobody realized—they couldn't get out of the water. The boat rode too high when it was empty. And it's such a big lake, they were too far from shore, and nobody came. . . ."

It seemed so unfair. A storm I could have understood, but—there was not a cloud in the sky. I remembered lying in bed sick with flu, thinking what a great summer day it was, what a good time everybody else was having. Probably somebody had yelled, "Last one in's a rotten egg!" And then they had all dived in without thinking. People having fun. Jumping in.

And then—realizing. I wondered sometimes what they had said to one another, what they had done. Whether they had been angry, or cried, or said good-bye.

Somehow I had stopped crying. "They all drowned," I told Chav almost calmly. "My father, my mother, my brother Adam, Uncle Dan, and little Cassie and Carrie."

His eyes were deep and wet, like the lake, letting me in—but it was all right, I would not drown in Chav. I could trust him. He was warm. His hand was warm on my shoulder.

I told him, "Sometimes I—sometimes I feel like, why did I live?"

"Good thing for me you did," Chav said softly.

That actually made me smile. But I said, "You know what I mean. Sometimes I feel like I should have been with them, I should have died. Or if it hadn't been for me, Liana would have been there on the boat to help us all back in the way she always did."

"Don't blame yourself," Chav said. "It wasn't your fault. Crap happens."

"It sure does."

"You're going to get over it."

"Yes." I knew I had to.

"You still just dive in anyway," Chav said. "That's good."

I stared at him, because I knew I was still scared of water—another thing I had to get over—and he knew it too, so what was he saying? There was a strange light-in-the-sky look on his face. His hand floated up off my shoulder, lifting like a wing.

"You take risks," he said slowly. "You haven't let

it—you won't stop loving. I think—it's better to—to love people, even if you get hurt."

It seemed kind of obvious to me, but it must have been important and new to him. His eyes had gone wide and shining, like he had seen God.

"You—you remember them," he said. "You had them while they were alive."

"Yes."

"I remember my mother. I—it's not such a bad deal."

"Yes. But, Chav, sometimes I feel—you know." Mad, sad, bad, the whole can of worms.

He did know. "You tell me when you're feeling that way, okay?"

"Okay."

"Promise?"

"Yes. I'll tell you if I feel awful." There had been times I couldn't tell Liana, she was hurting so much herself, but I could tell Chav, because he was strong.

Chav looked at me awhile longer, like he was trying to think of what else to say. But Angel was getting really restless, prancing under him, and that was okay. He asked me, "Do you want to canter?"

Actually, I did. All of a sudden I felt really good, light in the saddle, like I could ride forever. We cantered back up the meadow, and I dropped the reins and spread my arms, feeling the wind in my heart as well as my face. Chav looked at me and grinned and didn't say a word. He understood.

When we reached the top we slowed to a walk. Angel was way too skittish to take across the railroad bridge. We turned the other way, toward home.

"What are you going to do when you're out of school?" Chav asked me.

"I don't know yet." He should talk! This was the kid who barely believed in tomorrow. "Are you going out to the Spanish Dancer Ranch someday? See Rom again?"

"Maybe." A pause. "I'd like that." Another pause. "You know what else I'd like? Don't laugh."

"I won't. What?"

"I'd like to have my own place someday, you know, a farm, with all kinds of animals on it. Horses, ponies, donkeys, dogs, cats, bats, rats, wombats—"

Now he was trying to make me laugh. "Kangaroos," I suggested. "Gerbils." I had noticed there was no lack of gerbils lately.

"Yeah, gerbils, for sure. Hamsters. Hogs. Guinea pigs." For some reason he was smiling, a real smile that went clear to his eyes—they were starry bright. "Not just black animals," he said. "All colors."

I looked at him. "Black's nice," I said.

"I miss Rom," he said, "but Angel's going to be just as good someday." There was a wide-open clover field ahead of us. Chav tossed his forelock back from his eyes, ready for a gallop. "Hey hey, Gray! Let's go!" He sent Angel diving into the sunshine.

Nancy Springer has written a total of twenty fantasy novels and children's books. Her novels include *Not on a White Horse, They're All Named Wildfire, Red Wizard,* and *The Friendship Song,* all from Atheneum.

Ms. Springer teaches fiction-writing seminars at several Pennsylvania colleges. She is a communications instructor at Bradley Academy for the Visual Arts, a volunteer aide for Easter Seals 4-H Horseback Riding for the Handicapped, and a violinist with the York College of Pennsylvania Orchestra. An enthusiastic horseback rider, Ms. Springer depends on her Morgan mare, Avalong Finesse, to keep her out of trouble. She lives with her husband, Joel, their children, Jonathan and Nora, her shelty, Nicky, and too many gerbils in Dallastown, Pennsylvania.